RECLAMATION

Sister Mercy III

a novel by

Larry R. Macklin

RECLAMATION
Sister Mercy III

ISBN: 978-1-7330670-2-7

DEDICATION

Thank you to my friends who offered helpful suggestions and to my wife for her encouragement.

A special thank you to Keith Golay, PhD. Though you are no longer with us, what you've done for those needing support and encouragement will not be forgotten.

To the reader brave enough to take a chance on my writing, thank you. To all of you, my most sincere appreciation.

Larry R. Macklin
September, 2021

CHAPTER ONE

Keith Schwer woke up that morning grateful he had gotten the hay baled and into the barn before the storm blew through. The tornados which had ripped up the southwest portion of the state and parts of east Tulsa had been followed by a series of rain storms. It would seem things had almost dried out when another set of rain clouds would move in from the south and deluge things all over again. This had been going on for almost two months. They had already exceeded their annual average rainfall and it was only a little more than halfway through the year. No tornado or storm damage had harmed his farm northwest of Sapulpa, a suburb of Tulsa, but he knew folks on the east side of Tulsa hadn't been so lucky. He'd heard about similar problems in the southwest as well.

"Well, Ruthie, guess I need to get up and get at it. One more day without you, sweetie."

Keith was addressing the picture of his wife which sat on the night table next to the bed pancreatic cancer had forced her to vacate almost a year ago. He looked at the wall calendar. *Fifteen days until the anniversary of your passing and in three months it'll be our anniversary. I'm sorry, honey, but I'm not looking forward to either.*

He wiped away the escaping tear on his right cheek and shook himself back to the present.

Talking to himself, he said, "Come on, Keith boy. Today we're gonna move the cows to the north field, get 'em some hay and sunshine." He could have fed them hay in the barn but getting outside would be good for them, and good for him. Turning back to the photo, he added, "Oh, Ruthie, almost forgot to tell ya ol' Blackie somehow got in with the hens again. I swear that rooster gets craftier every day." He paused, then chuckled, "Remember when Doc' Steck prescribed some pills to boost my hormones and you started calling me 'Blackie'?" He was still chuckling as he put on his T-shirt and overalls, socks and well-worn work boots and headed out to do the daily chores.

He didn't *really* need to do any of it. He had sold some of the land and leased most of the rest. It was a very large farm he had inherited from his parents. When folks asked why he didn't just sell it off and go enjoy traveling and such he would just shake his head and say,

"What good would it be without Ruthie? 'Sides, this keeps me busy and right now I need that."

Of course, he wondered from time to time if the rest of his life was going to be a daily routine of chores until he either couldn't do them anymore or fell over dead trying. Now that his pain had subsided to a constant dull ache, he did wonder if a bit of excitement might make for a nice change every now and then. He stopped at the coffee pot set ahead to brew automatically and poured himself a steaming mug of the dark brown liquid. He took several sips as he looked out the kitchen window and thought aloud, "Excitement here? Ha, that's a good one."

He went to the bathroom and washed his face. *I'll take a shower before dinner. No point in doing it now when I'm just gonna get dirty and sweaty right away.*

Keith finished his coffee, put the mug in the sink, exited the kitchen's back door and took the path leading to the chicken coop. Once there, he scooped up a large coffee can full of feed from the grain bag in the storage cabinet next to the pen. Once grain was casted inside the fenced-in area, the chickens started clucking noisily as they pecked away.

"Yeah, you say you love me but I know what you *really* want," He joked. Sighing, he added, "Feed the chickens, slop the hogs, milk the cows. Just like every other day."

He only had three milk cows and four hogs, soon to be three since one of them was going to be turned into breakfast meat next week. Even so, with the chickens, he had more eggs, milk and bacon than he could handle. He and Ruthie hadn't had children, it just wasn't in the cards. The farm was their family. Now, it was a bachelor farm. He hated it, but at the same time, knew he needed it.

Once the chores were taken care of, Keith pulled his Dodge Ram pickup next to the barn. The Mechling brothers had come over to help him out with the hay baling and stacking. With the hay tucked into the loft, it meant he had to climb up to get at it, but it also meant he could drop the bales into the bed of the pickup below. He figured three bales should do it.

With that task completed he drove to the north field, pulled to a stop and opened the gate. He looked over the ground and it seemed to him like it'd dried out fairly well. He didn't want to risk compacting the soil so he decided he would drive near the fence. After he had gone a few hundred feet he noticed the cover for the hay ring had been blown off. It was laying on the ground about twenty yards further down. *After I get the ring feeder loaded, I'll pop it in the bed of the truck.*

As he approached the hay ring, he saw a dark lump at the base. It was almost black, and about the size of a soccer ball. *Maybe it IS someone's soccer ball. Don't know I've ever seen a black one before, but it could be I suppose, or maybe some animal whose misfortune caused it to be caught up by the storm. Hope it's not a skunk.* Keith honked the truck's horn several times. Whatever it was didn't move.

Keith exited the pickup, and proceeded to walk the remaining fifty feet to the object laying at the base of the iron hay ring. When he was within six feet it was clear whatever it was had hair or stringy fur.

He went back to the truck and took out the pitch fork he always carried when working with hay bales. Using the long-handled tined tool, Keith first poked, with no response, then moved the hard object to an open portion of the ring. Pushing it out into the open, he rolled it over. What he saw made him lose balance and fall backward. With eyes bulging, he got up and raced back to the truck and grabbed his cell phone.

"9-1-1, what is your emergency?"

"This is Keith Schwer, I need the sheriff to send someone out to my farm right away."

"Sir, can you state the nature of your emergency?"

"Someone died."

"Sir, how did you confirm they died? Did you check for a pulse or breathing?"

"NO, there was no need, please get the sheriff!"

"Sir, what do you mean there was no need?"

"IT'S A HEAD! IT'S SOMEBODY'S HEAD!"

CHAPTER TWO

Mark and Heather started their trip to town. It was the first time they were on a date and the first time as singles. Mark was apprehensive and excited and kept mentally admonishing himself for feeling like an adolescent. Heather was nervous thinking about Mark and how she would orient her life now the rope around her neck tying her to Roger Beaumont had been cut. *Well, cut legally if not physically.* There had been no further sign of Roger and no response to the many inquiries she and Mark had posted by means of the Service by Publication. Even so, there was still a nagging sense Roger had somehow escaped, in spite of all the evidence pointing to his demise.

Mark and Heather had mutually agreed to take things slow. For most new couples this would have meant dinner or going out to a movie, maybe including sodas and popcorn. For them it was going to be afternoon coffee at the Elkhorn Café. Mark thought to himself, *Slow is one thing but this is glacial.* Still, his gut was telling him Heather was the one and he ALWAYS trusted his gut. *It's going to take as long as it takes.*

"Mark?"

"Yeah?"

"Do you think Roger might have survived that storm…somehow?"

"Absolutely not."

Heather turned in her seat to face Mark, "How can you be so sure?"

Mark glanced at Heather, then returned his eyes to the highway, "Anyone who gets half their arm ripped off with barbed wire is not going to live to see the next sunrise. I don't care if they come from Alabama or not. Besides, it doesn't matter because I wouldn't let him get within a mile of you."

Heather loved Mark's protectiveness and concern. She might have joked that he was taking her on a cheap date but the depth of his caring made him just that much dearer and doing anything which might hurt his feelings was beyond consideration. *Wow, this is a world one hundred and eighty degrees from my previous life.* Heather wondered if she would get used to it but at the same time hoped she wouldn't. *I've never felt more special. First Sarah and now Mark.*

Maybe wishes DO come true.

Having arrived in Antelope Valley, they lucked out finding a parking space in front of the café. Mark killed the engine and Heather started to open the door to exit.

"Whoa, whoa, whaddya think your doin'?"

Heather looked at him surprised, "Huh, what do you mean?"

"Just hold your horses. I'm coming around to get you." Mark quickly hopped out, shut the door and hustled around the front of the vehicle. He pulled the door handle on Heather's door and then offered his other hand. Heather smiled and took his hand. She could have sworn a small jolt of electricity had traveled through her entire body.

Heather gathered her thoughts as she stood up, "Mighty gallant of you, sir."

"Beautiful ladies are worth it."

Was that another jolt of electricity?

Mark held the door of the café open. She stopped after taking a few steps into the restaurant.

Heather turned around and asked, "Do you have a favorite table you want to sit at?"

"The one that Heather Hollingsworth is at."

Gosh, if he doesn't stop doing that my hair is going to frizz!

Heather noticed that the table where Mark had eaten breakfast, when they first met, was open. Pointing, she asked, "Will this be okay?"

"Sure."

Neither had noticed that they were being observed by Mark's mother, Mabel. Mark's dad, Al, was busy in the kitchen with food preparation but Mabel wasn't helping. She had her eyes firmly glued on the couple. *A couple that might give us grandchildren ... finally. Wait! Don't get ahead of yourself there, Mabel. This is the first girl that Mark has been really serious about. You don't want to do anything to spook him.*

In spite of herself Mabel was on pins and needles. She had to release some of that energy. She walked over to Al who had his eyes set on the grill.

"Al, Mark is here with Heather!" she said in an excited whisper.

Al glanced up and then back down, "Yep."

"Oh, you old fart, you know this is exciting.

Exciting for our boy and exciting for us. Well, I'm hoping it's going to be exciting for us."

Al sighed, "Now, Mabel. Don't go messin' where your nose don't belong." Mixed metaphors seemed to have become a staple of Al's repertoire of late.

Mabel had returned to staring at the young couple, "Yeah, yeah." She picked up her order pad and started walking toward Mark and Heather. She proceeded past the only other customers in the place oblivious to their raised hands signaling for more coffee.

When she reached Mark and Heather's table, she said,

"Can I start you folks off with somethin' to drink?"

"Uh, mom, it's me, Mark and you *know* Heather. She works here?"

"Oh, mister smarty pants, I'm just bein' profesh'nal. So, how 'bout it? Want somethin' to drink?"

Heather smiled, "Sure, Mabel, thank you. Coffee, please."

Mabel turned to Mark, "And you?"

"Same for me, ma."

"Okay then, I'll get right on it."

Mabel turned and walked back to get the coffee urn, once again passing by raised hands without pause, grabbed the pot and returned. For a third time she passed by the customers which were now frantically trying to wave her down. She filled each of the young couple's cups, smiled and said,

"Now, if you need anything else, just flag me down."

Heather smiled, "Sure thing, Mabel, thank you."

As Mabel turned back, the customer she had disregarded spoke up,

"Mabel, what the sam hill does somebody need to do to get a refill?!"

"Earl, if you need somethin' you need to let me know!"

As Mabel filled his cup, Earl looked at his wife. No words were needed to figure out what he was thinking, *What the hell?*

Mabel returned the pot to the heater then

walked to the back of the restaurant where Al was still prepping for the dinner crowd. She walked up to him, grabbed his arm excitedly and shook it.

"Al, I saw them. They were holding hands!"

"COW POOP ON A STICK, MABEL! I'M STIRRIN' GRAVY HERE!"

Unfortunately, Al's voice carried well into the restaurant. Mark and Heather had no trouble in making out Al's words. Mark blushed and rolled his eyes. Heather nearly spit out her mouthful of coffee. Swallowing hurriedly, she then covered her smiling mouth with the napkin in her hand.

She looked at Mark who sighed and said,

"So, Ms. Hollingsworth, I take it you've met my family."

Heather's laugh echoed throughout the Elkhorn Cafe.

CHAPTER THREE

Mike Ahmadi, the former Muhammad Nabul, continued watching the woman breathing as she lay on the couch of her living room. He wondered at the wisdom of immediately showing her the photo of his father standing next to a much younger version of herself.

Of course, having lived in America all these years, he now knew the "Go Hoyas!" written by hand on the back of the photo referred to Georgetown University but that made the photo just the more puzzling.

His father had never mentioned Georgetown to him, let alone anything about this woman. When his father had asked him to find a 'Sarah Bennington' person, in America of all places, he had agreed. But the light had faded from his father's eyes before he could ask any questions. All he had left was a desire to stay alive and fulfill the fateful promise he had made to a dying father.

When the woman swooned at the sight of the photo, he had caught her before she could collapse to the floor. He had moved her to the couch, placed one of the small throw pillows there under her head, and then lifted her feet up onto the couch so she would be in a supine position. Checking her breathing and pulse, he knew CPR would not be necessary. He was relieved and puzzled. *Perhaps it's a heart condition and just not detectable without doing medical tests? This Sarah Bennington perso is an enigma. Was she really Sister Mercy from the news segment he had seen by chance? Maybe she has a twin sister. I suppose that's a possibility. I'll hope she's willing to tell me about my father and why they're in this photograph together. When she comes to I hope I can get answers to my questions.*

As if an answer to a prayer, Sarah Bennington moaned softly and, with a flutter of her eyes, started rising slowly to a sitting position. She noticed Mike sitting in the adjacent chair.

"Oh, dear," said Sarah, starting to swoon a bit.

"Ma'am, please take your time. I'm sorry if I upset you. Perhaps I could make you some tea?"

"That would be nice," replied Sarah, still feeling a bit groggy. She took a deep breath then pointed, "The kitchen is in that direction."

Mike rose and started toward the kitchen. Sarah called after him.

"The tea and small pot are in the top cupboard to the left of the sink."

Sarah heard the sound of cupboard doors opening and closing. *Was that the refrigerator?* Sarah called louder this time.

"What you need is in the top cupboard to the left of the sink."

Does the woman think I'm deaf? Mike had rummaged through the cupboard and had found the tea bags, and fortunately cardamom. He used a couple of cups of milk from the refrigerator and combined that in the pot with three tea bags. Two large serving spoons were used to sandwich and gently crush some cardamom seeds to release their flavor. After adding these to the milk and tea, he placed the pot on the stove. Noticing the matches in the wall dispenser, he lit the burner. After doing so, the hunt began for sugar.

"Are you okay in there?" shouted Sarah.

"Yes, it will be just a moment."

With gentle stirring, it only took five minutes

before Mike could see steam start to rise. After waiting a few more seconds, the burner was turned off and, using the wooden handles of the tea pot and its lid, he decanted the aromatic sheer chai into two cups. Having found the sugar hiding in the refrigerator, he added a teaspoon to each cup, stirring quickly. The spoon was laid in the sink and the pot returned to a cold burner on the stove. He picked up the cups and walked back to the living room.

"My goodness, what took you so long?"

"My apologies. Hopefully, you will find my favorite family recipe refreshing."

After taking the cup from the young man, Sarah took a sip and her eyes sprung wide open.

"It's been many years since I've tasted chai tea, especially sheer chai."

"So, you are familiar with this drink."

"Yes, … yes, I am familiar … ."

Mike noticed the woman seemed to be drifting away. *Is she going to faint again? Maybe the photograph will bring her around. If it causes her to faint once more, at least she's already on the couch.*

Pulling the photo once again from his pocket,

he asked, "Could you please explain to me about this photograph?"

"I'm sorry, but I've forgotten what you said earlier. How did you come to possess this picture, Mister-uh?"

"Ahmadi, but just call me Mike."

"Okay, Mike. Thank you. Now, about the photo?"

"My father gave it to me on the day of his death along with specific instructions to come to America and to find you. I do not know why he made the request. It's taken many years, and a lot of work, to accomplish that goal. I'm hoping you can explain. It *is* you in the picture?"

Sarah was feeling light-headed once again but managed to maintain her composure. "Mister Ah…, uh, Mike, would you mind telling me first how you came to arrive in America? I assume you traveled from Mazir-i-Sharif." *I need time to think. How will I tell him what he most certainly will not be ready to hear?*

How did this woman know this?! Mike was briefly stymied but quickly regained his composure.

"All right, but I do want to know about the photograph." Sarah nodded in reply. "What do you want to know about my journey?"

Sarah said, "Everything." Seeing his composure shift, she added with a raised hand, "I promise I will answer all of your questions after you are finished."

Mike sighed resignedly, paused for a moment, then with downcast eyes, muttered to himself, "Where to begin … where to begin?" Returning his gaze to Sarah, "I don't mean to upset you but it starts with the Taliban invading our city."

"This would be after the killing of the Taliban soldiers?"

How does this woman know these things?!

With a solemn nod, Mike Ahmadi began telling her his story. The same journey he had reminisced about in his apartment when he first beheld the face that, up to then, he had only seen in his father's photograph.

CHAPTER FOUR

Deputy Sheriff Sergeant Martin Acosta watched as the crime scene folks finished their work and began packing up the tools of their trade - preparing to head back to the forensics lab.

He had put together a team to go out to the farm after they had verified the farmer who had called it in wasn't a loon. Along with two subordinate Deputy Sheriff's, the field where the disembodied head had been found was canvased and then re-canvased again.

They had found nothing else to accompany or explain the half-denuded skull of some poor fellow. It looked to be male, somewhere in the thirty to forty age range, dark hair and eye color unascertainable. A ragged diagonal line ran from above the right eye to just above the left jaw line. Everything on the left side looked as if it had been stripped away with a scourge.

The only skin and flesh, if you could call it that, was on the right. Pocks in the skin, eyelids and most of the eye had been pecked or gnawed away. *The succession of rain storms these past weeks sure as hell didn't help either.* Acosta hoped a DNA test would reveal an identity to go along with the partial face. He didn't want this case dragging on. He had work to do helping LIVING people. *The poor sap, whoever he was, is way past that point. I've seen some crazy shit in my fourteen years as a deputy but this pretty much takes the cake.* He turned to the lead crime scene investigator,

"Hey, Tom, get a tissue sample over to OSBI and ask them to expedite a DNA search for this … cabeza."

Tom noticed he was pointing at the bagged head, "The last I heard, the Oklahoma State Bureau of Investigation had a backlog, but I'll see what I can do."

"Thanks." Then, mostly to himself, he said, "Time to go have a chat with the farmer."

Keith Schwer had been so shaken up when he showed them where to find the 'head', he'd had a difficult time talking to Acosta, let alone respond to his questions. The sergeant decided to have him go back to the farmhouse to pull himself together, with the admonishment to stay put until he could be interviewed. Keith had readily agreed.

On his return to his house, Keith entered the same door he had exited that morning. Puttering around in the bedroom, he started to tell Ruthie about it but thought, *No, no need to disturb her. I'll just let her rest in peace. I'll wait until I have something cheerful to share.* He decided finally to go to the kitchen and brew a cup of tea. Keith took the cup of steaming brew and sat at his kitchen breakfast table, sipping it slowly. He'd been jittery enough after his return. He didn't want to a jolt of caffeine from another cup of coffee to the mix. He closed his eyes and tried to think about the farm, the chickens, the pigs but still, the image of the human head refused to stop floating around in his mind. *I wonder if it will ever go away.* After taking another swallow of the reddish-brown liquid and nearly emptying the cup, He raised his eyes to look out the kitchen window. Deputy Sheriff Acosta was approaching the house. The image of the head floated to the front of his mind again. He waited for the knock. He didn't get up.

"Come on in, it's open." The deputy opened the door and poked his head inside.

"Mr. Schwer, how're ya doin'? Think you can

answer some questions?"

"I guess so." As the sheriff entered and closed the door, Keith asked, "Would you like something to drink? Coffee? Tea?"

Taking a small spiral note pad and pen from his shirt pocket, Acosta said, "No, no, I'm fine but thanks for asking." He pulled out the chair opposite the farmer and sat down, removing his cowboy hat and setting it on the table.

"You've got a nice place. How long you been farming here?"

Keith gave a small shrug, "All my life up to almost a year ago. That's when my wife passed away."

"I'm very sorry to hear that. Please accept my condolences."

"Thanks. I'm starting to learn to deal with it. Don't have much choice …", his voice trailed off.

The deputy cleared his throat, "The lab guys tell me that the head found in your field had to have been there for quite some time. How come you only came across it yesterday?"

"With my wife gone, and the fact that, over time, I've leased most of my farmland … fact is, it's really just a hobby farm for me anymore. I was getting set to move my few milk cows over to that field, mainly to just have something to do. The last thing in the world I expected was to find what I did. I called 9-1-1 immediately."

"We appreciate that. So, you didn't notice any unusual activity on or around your farm before yesterday?"

"No, in fact I was telling my wife …"

The deputy interrupted, "Your wife? I thought you said she passed away."

Keith's right eye started to tear up, "She did", he blushed, "but I still talk to her."

It was the deputy's turn to feel uncomfortable, "I … see." After a brief pause, "So, you didn't notice anything else around your farm, pieces of clothing, tools that might have been left out when the storms passed through, or …"

"No, nothing. In fact, I was telling Ruthie …," Keith paused to use the last sip of tea to clear the lump in his throat, "that nothing exciting happens around here, that it's the same day after day. I had no idea how prophetically wrong I was going to be." Once again, the ghoulish image of the head plagued his mind.

After looking at the words on his notepad, which could be counted on one hand, Acosta let out a small sigh. Closing the notepad and clicking his pen, he returned both items to his shirt pocket. Reaching into the opposing pocket, he pulled out a business card. He picked up his hat, placed it firmly on his head and then handed the card to Keith.

"If something comes to mind or you find anything else that might be related, however trivial, feel free to give me a call." He paused for a moment, "Or, if you just want to chat, that'll be okay as well."

For the first time in many weeks, Keith's mouth curled into a small smile, "That's nice of you. Thank you for the offer."

"Sure thing. I'll show myself out. Take care Mr. Schwer."

"You as well, deputy." With that, Acosta left, closing the door behind him and walked to the departmental SUV he had driven out to the farm.

After getting in, shutting the door and placing the key in the ignition, he muttered, "What a crazy ass nightmare to happen to such a nice guy."

* * *

When the call came in, it was Mark Stoner who picked up the phone, "Hello, Antelope Valley Police Department, how can I help you?" Sergeant Mike Glatt was at his desk reviewing notices. He looked up to see Mark's face fall.

"Okay, Mrs. Riley, we'll be over in a few minutes. You really need to get that fence fixed so your cow can't get out. Yes. Yes. Okay, then, see you in a few minutes."

Mike said, "Want me to go over there?"

Mark's answer was immediate, "Not on your life. Sitting around here is driving me crazy. This will only take twenty minutes or so but it's probably the only excitement we'll see today."

Mike gestured a 'whatever' as Mark left the office. Mike got up and walked to the break room to get a cup of coffee. When he started to pick up the glass pot off the burner, he could smell the foul sludge that was clinging to the bottom.

"Damn it, Mark, it wouldn't kill you to clean the pot once in a while." The only response was the sound of the office door closing followed a minute later by the muffled sound of the department's cruiser being started.

Mike cleaned the pot, wishing he could hold his nose at the same time. Once it was in decent shape, he added water to the maker, replaced the filter and then added several scoops of fresh grounds. Punching the start button, he leaned back against the counter, folded his arms and waited as the hot brown liquid started its gurgling journey to the glass orb.

Mike had just sat back down with his coffee when Mark Stoner returned to the office. Mark hung up his weather breaker and then plopped his campaign hat on his desk as he took his chair.

"So, Officer Stoner, did Mrs. Riley's cow give you any trouble? Resisting arrest, anything like that?"

"Ha, ha," replied Mark, "at least I'm not getting splinters in my butt sitting at a desk all morning."

"Yeah, not exactly exci …," Glatt snapped up straight in his chair, "…ting." After a brief pause, he added, "You're not going to believe this."

Mark rose from his desk and ambled over to Glatt's desk to peer over the sergeant's shoulder at the computer monitor. "Whassup?"

Glatt snickered, "Workin' on your street cred, are ya? Says here that the sheriff's department over in Creek County found a man's head with no body attached."

Mark stood up from his leaning position, "So?"

"So? ... SO?! Don't you think this might be related to the arm we came across?"

"Mike, come on, that is such a stretch. How far is it to-o-o, what's the nearest town to that location, Sapulpa?"

"Well, I don't know." Glatt decided to open a Chrome window and search for distance using Google Maps. After a few moments he announced, "Says here that it's 246 miles. But, keep in mind, that's driving distance. It would be shorter, as the crow flies."

"Okay, even if I give you a large margin for that, you're talking about a man's arm and head separated by 200 miles. Face it. It's two people and two different deaths. Well, one likely death and one confirmed. Did it say anything else?"

"No, just that they're hoping to get an ID by searching the DNA test results through the Combined DNA Index System, you know, CODIS. That's pending."

Mark walked slowly back to his desk, "Yeah, I know, but don't hold your breath. By the way, if you're looking for excitement, the next time Mrs. Riley's cow breaks through her fence, *you* can go corral it."

Mike Glatt didn't respond, instead he picked up the handset to his desk phone and punched a speed-dial number.

"Yes, may I please speak to Doc, er, Doctor Simpson? Yes, tell him it's Sergeant Mike Glatt."

After suffering through two minutes of elevator music a voice came on the line, "Hello, Michael, how are you doing? Need something?"

"Hey, Uncle Paul, sorry to bother you but I was wondering if you guys submitted the DNA results from that arm we brought you?"

"I'm sure we did. Let me just check, hang on." Glatt heard an intercom 'bong' and his uncle's barely audible voice asking someone name Terry if the sample had been submitted to the national DNA database. This was followed by a 'thank you' and the return of his uncle's voice on the phone, "Yes, I just confirmed with our senior technician that it was loaded to the CODIS database. Keep in mind that technically we had to identify it as a 'John Doe' pending ID confirmation."

"Okay, thanks."

"That it? What's going on?"

"Oh, well, you can file this under 'stranger than fiction', but the sheriff over in Creek County managed to find a head with no body. They're waiting on results from CODIS."

"And you think the arm and head might be related?"

"I know, I know, it's a wild stretch. Two different pieces of a body being found so far apart…"

"It's very, very likely to be a coincidence, you know that, right, Michael?"

"Yeah, yeah. But just from an academic point

of view do you think it's *possible* for a human head to be carried that far by a tornado?"

"Well, if asking about a possibility, that would be about … 200 plus miles I would guess. I suppose it's *possible*. If you're asking about probability, I'd say if it turns out you're correct, it's time to snatch up some lottery tickets. Anything else?"

"No, no. Sorry I took up your time."

"Not a problem. Good to hear from you. Next time, maybe give me a call before another month goes by, or you find a member missing a body."

"Okay, okay, will do, Uncle Paul. Bye."

"Bye."

Mark looked up at Glatt as he put the handset back in it's cradle. "What'd he say?"

"That if it turns out I'm right, that the arm and head are from the same person, I should go out and buy lottery tickets."

"See?"

"Yeah. It's just that it bugged me for some reason when I read about it. Oh, well, back I go to splinterville."

CHAPTER FIVE

Mike Glatt looked up at the station's wall clock. *Oh my god, is it really only 4:30?* The coffee time Mark had with Heather seemed to go by in a flash. Now, the afternoon seemed to be dragging on forever. *How is it a half day off goes by in the blink of an eye and the other half at work is unending? The* only excitement today had belonged to Mark Stoner. *How sad is it that rescuing a cow is the highlight of our day?*

"You planning on heading home soon?"

Mark looked up and said, "Naw, I told Heather I would pick her up from work. She isn't due to get off until after the dinner rush, so…" , looking at his watch, "probably around seven or so. You?"

"Yeah, I think I'll boogie at five. Say, you're getting mighty friendly with this gal. Should I be planning on renting a tux anytime soon?"

He thought Mark would smile at the quip but instead he leaned back in his chair and looked thoughtful. After a moment he spoke up.

"To tell you the truth, Mike, I'm not sure. That asshole of a husband she had really screwed things up good. Guess he screwed me too because she's … she's … I don't know, spectacular, delicate, wonderful, unsure …?"

Mark's hands had started creating circles. Glatt figured he was at a loss for words or else the poor young man was having a conniption fit.

Glatt raised an eyebrow and said, "Sounds like you're pretty hung up on this girl." Mark just sighed and nodded.

Glatt asked, "So, what's your plan?"

Mark shrugged, "I wish I knew. I know I'm ready to leap right in but I'm pretty sure she isn't. All I know is, when I'm with her, I'm happier than I've ever been. I guess it means I've decided to commit to however long it takes for us to be together."

Glatt turned serious, "Mark, you are one hell of a good man. She'll see that in time. You'll see."

Mark gave the sergeant a small smile, "Thanks, Mike, nice of you to say."

"It's also why I won't let her see me, you know, in case you suffer by comparison."

Mark laughed, then picked up a wad of paper and threw it at Mike, "Shut up, you jerk!"

Glatt made a mock show of horror, ducking the impotent projectile, just as the captain walked in.

The captain took turns looking at them both, "Are you two going to be playing footsies next?"

Glatt stood at attention, saluted, and said, "Absolutely not, sir, everyone knows about Stoner's contagious case of athlete's foot."

The captain smiled while Mark just shook his head, "That was actually kind of funny, Mike. Both of you heading out?"

Glatt was the first to speak, "Yeah, Cap, in just a bit."

The captain turned toward Mark with a raised eyebrow. Mark sat up and said, "I'm going to hang around here until around seven. I told Heather I would give her a ride home."

The captain nodded, "That's the new gal at the Elkhorn Café, right?" Mark nodded. "She seems real nice. You two are starting to become something of an item around town. Hope things work out for you both." After a pause, he added, "Okay then, Mark, make sure you lock up and clean the coffee pot, yes?" Mark acquiesced with a raised hand. "All right, you two, see you tomorrow ... unless Mrs. Riley's cow gets out again," the captain left chuckling.

After the captain was gone, Mike Glatt starting organizing his desktop - putting pens away and filing what few papers he had. He got up and shoved the desk chair in, gave the desk one more glance, then walked over and gave Mark's shoulder a pat.

Mark responded with, "See ya manana, Mike."

Glatt smiled, "Not if I see you first."

"Ha, ha. Take care, buddy."

Glatt responded with a sincere, "You too. Hope things work out for you and Heather."

"Thanks. Appreciate it."

With a wave, Glatt said, "See ya."

After Glatt closed the office door, Mark leaned back and put his feet up on his desk. He would try to think of a plan for a future with the lady he was more and more sure he was falling in love with. "With WHOM I am falling in love," he muttered to himself smiling, thinking of his high school English teacher, Mrs. Herron. He didn't really expect any results from his cogitation but the effort might help him fill the two hours he would be waiting until he could be with her, alone, once more.

*　*　*

Mark didn't think there was any way two hours could last as long as it did but after he had cleaned the coffee pot, arranged his desk, found Mike Glatt's deck of Bicycle playing cards and lost eight hands of solitaire, he was finally close enough to Heather's quitting time to lock up and drive over to the café.

Mark still didn't have any real plan, as far as their relationship went, other than the old standby 'play it by ear'. Still tossing things around in his mind, he realized that, somehow, he was now approaching the Elkhorn. He pulled into a spot just a few spaces down from the café's front door. His watch indicated that he was a quarter hour early. *Not so bad. At least waiting here is a change of scenery.* Mark leaned back in the seat and waited, periodically looking out the driver side window. Twenty minutes later, Heather exited through the café doors. Just the sight of her made him smile. She stopped to reach her arms straight up and bend backwards to stretch her back. He couldn't stop himself from noticing the gentle rise and descent of her breasts as she did this. He thought the temperature in the car must be rising a little bit. Brushing a stray strand of hair from her forehead, she turned to look for him and spotted him instantly. With the recognition came a warm smile.

He mumbled, "Markie, boy, you are in over your head with this lady." He started to exit the car but Heather waved him back.

After she got in she said, "Hi, Mark. Thanks for the ride."

"No problem, ready to go?"

"Well, not really."

"Huh? Why not?"

"I called Sarah earlier to remind her you were giving me a ride today. She said that, right after we left, she had company arrive from out of town. She didn't say anything further but I think she wanted some private time and I don't want to intrude. Would it be okay if we hung around town for a while? Maybe make it back around … 10 pm or so?"

Stoner thought for a moment, "Well, why don't we drive over to Bayer and see what's playing at the Stovall theater? My treat."

Heather smiled, "Sounds like fun. Okay."

Mark said, "Well, their ICEE machine will give you a horrific brain-freeze and they put so much salt in their popcorn, you'll swell up like a weather balloon, so, yeah, fun."

That made Heather laugh. She playfully pushed on his shoulder with her hand. It felt like grabbing a rock. She was smiling but also thinking the temperature in the car must be rising a little bit.

CHAPTER SIX

Mike Ahmadi had to clear his throat several times. Not because he needed it to speak, but instead to give himself a few seconds to gather his thoughts. This enigmatic lady, who apparently not only knew his father but other information as well, which seemed inexplicable, had asked him about his life, his journey and how he came to arrive in America. It was clear, if he wanted answers as to why his father wanted him to find her, he needed to acquiesce to her request.

"Well," he said, "to start, I was raised in Mazir-i-sharif. That's in northern Afghanistan."

The woman nodded, "I'm aware."

How does a simple farm woman know about Afghanistan? "My father became mayor of the city and we had a good life. A good life, that is, until the problem with the Taliban started."

The woman was nodding once again but said nothing. This caused Mike to pause briefly but then he continued, "The year before my father and sister were killed, Taliban soldiers tried to take over our city. There was intense fighting but we were prepared and most of the soldiers were killed or captured. I don't know what happened to those who were captured."

Sarah nodded slightly but thought, *I have a pretty good idea.*

Mike continued, "I remember seeing road equipment, bulldozers, backhoes, that kind of heavy road machinery being driven down the street past our house. At the time, I didn't know why but, this many years later, I have a strong suspicion they were used for mass graves. What followed that event was a tenuous cease-fire. Of course, there were periodic stories of someone being shot outside the city but this was me overhearing adults talk with my twelve-year-old ears."

Mike stopped. Recalling the story had made his throat tighten. He took a sip of the chai tea he had prepared earlier. He watched as Sarah did the same.

"How is it you are familiar with sheer chai?"

"Your father introduced me to it."

Mike raised an eyebrow, but Sarah pretended she didn't notice, "Please go on."

Setting his cup down, Mike Ahmadi

continued, "There were negotiations over what seemed like many months. I remember my father getting upset and sometimes speaking his frustrations aloud. He was fearful of the Taliban. He kept receiving news they were building up for an offensive to take over the city in spite of their talks about a peaceful agreement.

In late summer, the year my father and the rest of my family were killed, I overheard him speak with some city officials and religious leaders. They discussed an agreement proposed by the Taliban. The Taliban would seize control of the city but would not seek revenge for the killing of their soldiers. In return, all of our soldiers and weapons had to be removed from Mazir-i-Sharif before the Taliban arrived. My father said it seemed to be a reasonable solution given the overwhelming odds the city would face otherwise."

Sarah closed her eyes. She knew full well the outcome of the agreement. Sarah opened her eyes again as Mike Ahmadi proceeded with his story.

"I get the feeling I'm not telling you much of anything new. Can you please explain how you came to be in a photograph with my father and why you know so much about Mazir-i-Sharif?"

Sarah thought for a second. *Well, I might as well just talk. I can't think of any best way to share what will surely be unexpected, if not shocking, news for this young man.*

"Your father and I met in college. I attended high school here, in Antelope Valley but while in high school my parents were both killed in a terrible car accident."

Sarah gestured around herself briefly, "I had to come here to live with my grandparents. Life was thrown totally upside down for me. I was fortunate to be a good student scholastically and got accepted to a number of good colleges and universities, but I wanted to get as far away from here as I could. So, when I was accepted at Georgetown, I chose that particular university because it was as far East as I could go. Of course, my grandparents were disappointed but I think they knew the memory of my folks had plagued me ever since the accident. The nightmares had subsided but never truly went away. It was my hope that a completely different environment might offer me an escape, fresh air, a way to focus on the future rather than being smothered by the past. It turned out it didn't really. Not, that is, until I met your father."

Mike Ahmadi scooted forward slightly while Sarah took a sip of tea. It helped her throat but it didn't help her emotions.

"My first year at Georgetown was difficult but also pleasant. The other students, the professors, everyone was so nice. They treated you with dignity and respect. It was so different from high school, especially a small-town high school. No cliques to mark you as an outsider. At Georgetown, if you didn't fit in with a group, there were a plethora of others to choose from. Initially, I found making my way around campus and arranging my classes very challenging. I had money for school tuition, books and living expenses but virtually nothing extra. I had to be very frugal. So, I took a part-time job in a grocery store in the summer which helped familiarize me with the local neighborhood and financed forays into the surrounding community. By the time my second year was underway, I was much more comfortable with the environment but also homesick. The excitement of being in a new place had faded and my reminiscing about this home brought back the bad dreams."

Mike was fidgeting, "I see, but how does this relate to my father?"

"Please be patient, I'm getting there."

CHAPTER SEVEN

Tom Burrton was going over marijuana identification with a forensic lab trainee,

"The problem we're faced with here is, taxonomically, marijuana and hemp are one and the same plant, *Cannabis sativa*. Of course, if you look at the whole plant side by side, you can see anatomical differences and know one is marijuana and the other hemp. Take it from me , you will never see a whole plant unless they take down a grower and, since it's illegal to cultivate either plant, you won't be needed for an identification."

The trainee asked, "So, do we do DNA testing?"

Tom snorted, "Hell, no, that's expensive." He paused then continued, "When you get … material that is suspected of being marijuana, you have to first confirm that it's not something else that might be legal."

The trainee frowned, "What could that be?"

Tom smiled, "Believe it or not, some knucklehead got stopped and the sheriff found a bag of what looked like weed in his pocket. Turned out the idiot paid thirty bucks for oregano."

They both laughed at that. "Okay, so what's the procedure?"

Tom motioned him over to the microscope at his workstation, "Well, other than the characteristics that are generally found on all plants like covering hairs, and others, There are two structures. One is called a cystolithic trichome and the other a glandular trichome. Take a look in the microscope and see if you can find a claw like structure.

The trainee took a second and then said, "Yep, got it."

"That's the cystolithic trichome and the bulbous base is rich in calcium carbonate, again, a feature common to many plants. Now see if you can spot a rosette-shaped head on top of a multi-cellular stalk."

"Um, not sure, oh, there, yeah, I see it."

"That's the glandular trichome and it's responsible for secreting cannabinoids. Look …"

"Hey, Tom." Tom's instructive session was interrupted by Susan, another forensic lab analyst.

"Yeah?"

"There's a Deputy Acosta on the phone for ya. Says it's important."

"Okay, be right there." Turning to the trainee, he said, "So, what you've learned is that we can identify what may or may not be marijuana but which, at least, raises suspicion of being a controlled substance. Once we haven't eliminated other sources outright, we do a Duquenois-Levine screening test. You can find it in the procedure manual. Read up on it while I'm on the phone."

"Is it definitive for cannabinoids?"

Tom shook his head, "No, it has a significant level of false positives. But, it is cheap. If the case would warrant it we would move forward with Thin Layer Chromatography. That too is qualitative but very specific and not cheap. To really nail it down we'd need G.C. – Mass Spec. You'll get trained on that further down the road. Gotta go."

Tom walked over to the nearest multi-line lab phone, "Burrton here."

"Hey, Tom. Have you heard anything from OSBI about the DNA test on the head we found a while back?"

"No, and I'm sorry Martin, I've been real busy and forgot to follow up with them. I'll give them a call to see where they're at and then give you a shout, okay?"

"All right. Just trying to get some of the case-load crap closed. Thanks."

"Okay, I understand. I'll call you later."

"10-4."

Tom walked back over to his trainee.

"I need to ask you something, Tom. If almost all of this is presumptive, how do they get convictions if we can only prove that it *might* be cannabis?"

"Well, that's the funny thing about the law and when politics override science. Law enforcement assumes that it is a controlled substance. The suspect knows whether it is or not … with some notable exceptions." They both smiled at the earlier reference. "So, it becomes a case of guilty until proven innocent."

"Wow, that doesn't sound fair."

"No one, my friend, can claim that life is fair. Keep reviewing procedures, I'm going to check on the status of the horseless headsman."

"The *what*?"

"Oh, forgot that you hadn't heard about that. Farmer a little ways west of here found a man's head, or what was left of it, laying in a field on his farm. It was pretty gruesome. We sent it over to OSBI for a DNA check to see if it's owner could be identified."

"Holy crap on a biscuit."

"Yeah. I'll be back in a couple minutes."

Burrton left and proceeded to the break room to get a cup of coffee. He decided to use his cellphone. He had Nadene's number in his contacts and knew she would either know or help expedite things if the test was delayed. She would be key to getting Acosta off his ass. He poured the hot brown liquid into his cup while holding the phone in his other hand close to his ear. He heard it ringing. as he sat down at one of the break tables.

"Hello? Tom?"

"Hey, Nadene. How's the family?"

"Well, my husband still leaves his socks on the floor and my 8-month old is teething like crazy. I tried your idea of cotton balls soaked in bourbon and it worked great but I think little Billy is enjoying it too much. Gonna have ta cut him off the sauce and get real medicine. So, what's up?"

Tom chuckled and asked, "Did you guys find out anything about that head on CODIS?"

"Oh, yeah, the freak show. I'm at my workstation, give me a sec to look it up. Boy, that was a weird one, huh?"

"You said it." Tom could hear the key clicks. He had just swallowed a sip of coffee when she spoke again.

"Well, do you want the bad news or the crazy news?"

What the hell? "Uh, give me the bad news first."

"Your head did get a hit. The problem is, it's a John Doe."

"Okay, so, what's the crazy news?"

"The hit was for a dismembered forearm and hand."

"Really? I didn't hear anything about you guys being sent an arm."

"Oh, we didn't do the work. It wasn't from here."

"Okay, I think you're going to tell me the crazy part, right?" Tom started to take another sip of coffee.

"Yes. The hand and arm DNA was recorded from the medical center located in Antelope Valley, more than 200 miles southwest of here."

Tom choked on the mouthful of coffee he had started to swallow.

"Are you shitting me?!"

"Nope. I'm reading it right here. There's also a note that says the Antelope Valley police want to be notified on any updates regarding identity. It says to call a sergeant Mike Glatt. There's nothing here stating that's been done. That's it.

"Okay, Nadene, thanks a lot. I think."

"Sure, Tom. Good luck with … whatever."

Tom disconnected without responding. Either someone made a huge mistake or something unbelievable actually happened. It didn't matter because the only way to identify the head now was to have forensic reconstruction done and pray that someone, somewhere could recognize the person. He wondered if Acosta had money in his budget for a facial reconstruction job on that head and figuring out who it was. *He's gonna shit a brick!*

CHAPTER EIGHT

Mike Ahmadi could see the woman, Sarah, was agitated. He started feeling sorry he had pressed her about the photo. Maybe a diversion would help her relax a little.

"You know, I had nightmares for a while myself as I made my way from Afghanistan."

He noticed this comment got Sarah's attention.

"How did you do it? And, at such a young age. It couldn't have been easy."

Mike nodded and smiled slightly, "Well, true, but then I was too young and naïve to know that I shouldn't have been able to. I traveled south to Pakistan and then along the Iranian border. I walked and hitched rides which ended in Chabahar. When I realized I had somehow reached a coastal area, I was excited. I couldn't believe my luck at having arrived at a coastal city by the Gulf of Oman. My plan was to somehow make it to the UAE and find work. This, I hoped, would eventually allow me to purchase travel to America." Smiling, he added, "It was as far as my teenage brain had strategized by that point."

Sarah marveled at the resourcefulness this young man must have possessed. She shook her head ever so slightly. Mike noticed.

"And my father?"

Sarah shook her head again and with a small wave of her hand said, "Please, tell me first how a penniless young teenage boy manages to cross a gulf in the middle east!"

Mike let out a small sigh and rubbed the old scar on his right hand, "Well, it involves a fishing boat captain who saved my hand at the last split second. I'm not going to go into the details behind that, but let's just say he made me work my passage off on his boat until it dropped anchor near Sohar."

"Sohar in Oman?"

This lady is an enigma. "Yes, but the boat itself didn't dock. I was ordered to board another vessel. It was owned by a very rich man, Arab, I seem to recall. Anyway, the rich man took me by way of a small motor craft to the docks where I was told to get in a large black automobile. He and his driver, a dark, quiet, scary sort, were aloof and gave away little. The rich man seemed to be treating me nicely. I didn't understand why he would do that, but I had and still have suspicions about it. From there we drove to Dubai and then boarded a private jet which went to Germany first but ultimately arrived in the United States at Logan Airport in Boston. It was beyond my wildest dreams to have arrived in America this way and so quickly."

Sarah's hand flew to her mouth. Her eyes could not have opened wider. This was not the second time she had beheld her son. It was the third.

Mike Ahmadi was taken aback. "Are you okay? Was it something I said?"

Sarah nodded. She held up her other hand and took several deep breaths.

With a concerned look on his face, Mike asked, "What is it?"

Sarah gathered herself, "It turns out we *have* met each other before."

His look of concern shifted to doubt, "I … don't think so. I would have remembered…"

"Do you remember Mr. Smith calling on Archbishop Hamlin?"

Now it was Mike's turn to look astonished,

"How could you possibly know about that!?"

"I was the novitiate, the nun, who talked to you." Then, in Pashto she added,

"Hello. What is your name?"

Mike fell backward against the couch with his mouth open. After a moment he gathered himself and asked, "That was you?! You, who presented me to the lady that found a family to take me in?"

With a tear forming in her eye, Sarah nodded affirmatively.

"Yes, yes, it was me." After a brief pause she added, "Now, let me tell you more about how I came to know your father." *God in Heaven, please let him hear and understand my words. Or, better yet, hear and accept my words. You've turned your back on me in the past. I'm expecting better of you now.*

CHAPTER NINE

Mark and Heather parked on the street half a block away from the Stovall Theatre. After locking the car, they strolled side by side to the first of two billboards advertising a 'Coming Attraction'. Neither took notice as they were both focused on each other. Heather noticed that the theatre was small, like *really* small. It had two auditoriums. The last time she had been to a movie in Kansas City was at a multi-plex. *It had sixteen theatres, or was it eighteen? And the movies were current!*

Mark said, "Well, let's see what's playing. Probably should've called ahead."

"Best laid plans," replied a smiling Heather.

God she is cute. Mark looked up at the postings behind the ticket taker, a cute blond girl of high school age with a sprinkling of freckles across the bridge of her nose between sparkling blue eyes.

"Can I help you, sir?"

Mark couldn't believe that someone was now referring to him as 'sir'.

"Just need a minute." Turning to Heather, he said, "What do you think?"

Heather looked at the titles, one to an old comedy and the other a middle-aged romantic comedy. It was "Just Like Heaven". That was the last movie Heather had seen before marrying Roger so it was the last movie she had seen … period.

Heather pointed at the second one, "How about that one, 'Just Like Heaven'. Would that be okay?" She felt a little guilty pretending she didn't really know about it. It was a fun romance movie. It had funny parts but the two people who belonged together overcame humongous odds and ended up in each other's arms. It was something she used to dream about but never experienced. *Well, at least not yet.*

Mark nodded, "Fine by me." *Man, I hope it's not some syrupy slobbering love story.* Turning to the cashier, he said, "Two adults for Just Like Heaven."

After running his card and handing him the tickets, the cashier said, "The movie doesn't start for another twenty minutes. They should be through cleaning up the theatre in about five or so and then you can go in."

Mark took a step back and looked right.

Hansen's Furniture store was open. He turned to Heather, "We could go next door and browse a while until it's nearer time for the movie."

Heather nodded, "Sounds great, let's."

Without either of them being conscious of it until after it happened, they entered the store holding hands. Both appeared to be looking around but both had their minds focused on the feeling of the other's touch.

They had passed by the living room furniture section of the store and had just started to enter the bedding section when a salesman approached.

"Can I help you folks find a bed?"

Mark's brain froze. Heather blushed and stammered slightly and finally blurted out, "Um, no, we're not married."

"Oh, sorry, you two looked like a married couple. My mistake. Well, if you need any help finding anything, just let me know, but be aware that we close in half an hour."

Mark's brain and tongue finally came loose, "Er, uh, yeah, we're just browsing until the movie starts but if we need anything, we'll let you know."

The man winked and gave Mark a thumbs up.

Mark looked at his watch, "It's been ten minutes. How about we go freeze your brain and salt you down before the movie starts?"

Heather giggled and clutched Mark's arm, "Okay, it's a deal."

They exited the store and walked back to the theatre's entrance. After handing over the tickets and getting the torn halves handed back, they proceeded to the concession stand. They were met by a somber, pimply-faced teenager who couldn't have been older than sixteen.

"Can I help you, sir?"

There's that 'sir' again, and did that kid's voice just crack? Mark looked at Heather, "ICEE and popcorn?"

Heather smiled, "I hear it's a unique experience." That made Mark grin.

Turning to the kid he said, "You heard the woman."

"What flavor, sir?"

Mark looked at Heather. She perused the ICEE machines and said,

"Something that will turn our tongues blue."

CHAPTER TEN

Sarah paused briefly to gather her thoughts. *I want to be frank and as truthful as possible about everything but I pray my composure holds. My painful past has been something I've spent many years trying to forget.*

"I decided to pursue a double-major at Georgetown, Comparative Religion and Mid-Eastern Studies. It took me an extra year. I then decided to pursue a Master's Degree in Arabic Studies. I concurrently enrolled in the graduate certificate program for Refugee and Humanitarian Emergencies. It was during this time that I met your father. He was enrolled in the certificate program for International Business Diplomacy.

There were several classes that overlapped and we noticed each other in the first class we shared and then discovered we were in a class together again the following semester. I remember the professor in that class cracking a joke regarding Dari and Farsi being, in an upside-down sort of way, like England and America – having two languages separated by a common country. Of course, while humorous, the juxtaposition doesn't apply to Pashto since it's a separate language entirely, having similar words and sharing the same culture and alphabet. Since most major cities in Afghanistan host both languages, it was explained that education is provided to kids in their native language and they start studying either Pashto or Dari as a second language in the 4th grade. Your father was a native Pashto speaker so Dari was a second language for him."

Mike appeared to be getting antsy. *Well, he needs to be patient.*

"After the second semester, we were like two magnets. We kept bumping into each other even though we no longer had classes in common. His schedule had him coming to a building as I was leaving and vice versa. It almost seemed fated. We started chatting almost every day. He would mentor me in Pashto at the library once a week."

Sarah paused, "Such a handsome man. I was quite taken with him. I wanted him to ask me out and thought he never would but then, when I had almost given up hope, he finally invited me to dinner. This progressed to the point where we were doing something together almost each weekend. We went to sporting events with our student passes. That's when the photo you showed me was taken. Those were wonderful days." *Until ...*

Sarah could tell her emotions were starting to get away from her. She needed to stop for a moment to calm herself down.

"Can I take a break?" Before Mike could respond she added, "Would you mind telling me about your life after the family took you in?"

This is taking forever, thought Mike Ahmadi. *I guess I'd better go along or else she might shut down entirely and this whole trip will have been a waste.*

"All right," said Mike, "well, the family who took me in and eventually adopted me were Syrian, I don't know if you knew that."

Sarah didn't move. She had forgotten but his comment brought back the discussion the social worker had over the phone the day Sarah left a young Afghani boy in her care. Apparently, his remedial English either hindered him or else he didn't hear or remember it mentioned.

Mike assumed Sarah's non-response meant no. *Well, finally, something this woman DOESN'T know.*

"It turns out they were Syrian Christians. I imagine that may be why they got out of Syria and immigrated to the U.S. Anyway, it was a difficult transition although they did accommodate my Islamic customs. I sat through their insistence on grace during meals and they put up with my daily prayers. At first, I didn't get along with their youngest son, Karam, who was a year younger than me.

"He was a slender, sort of bookish boy. Unfortunately, that made him a target for bullies. One day, he was cornered in the school yard by three boys. Typical cowardice of bullies, they never fight one on one. I happened to be walking by and saw them taunting him, trying to pull away his back-pack, demanding, I believe, money. I yelled at them in Pashto, 'Leave him alone!'

"My shout drew their attention away from Karam and they started walking toward me. I had picked up some fighting skills during my journey to the Gulf of Oman. I didn't wait for them to start anything. After taking care of two, the one still standing, the bully, drew back his fist but then paused when he felt the blade of my pen knife against his nose. I invited him to never bother my brother or me again. He accepted."

"Karam must have told his parents about the encounter at school because, from that point on, I was treated like a true son in their family. As Karam and I became closer, it was an ironic circumstance I was good at math and poor at English while he was exactly the opposite. We started tutoring each other at home. Karam and I are still good friends to this day."

Sarah realized she had been leaning forward as Mike told his story. She slowly leaned back a little and asked, "Did you finish high school? Pursue a college degree?"

Mike nodded, "Yes, yes I did. I was not the head of my high school class but I did well enough to be accepted to Boston College where I majored in Accounting and minored in Business Communications."

Sarah said, "Remarkable. So, what are you doing now? For work, I mean."

"I'm a tax policy analyst for the Internal Revenue Service. Finding work after 9-11 was very difficult. Even though I've been told my accent sounds Bostonian, if anything, the color of my skin was not considered … suitable for employment. I had hoped to get a job at one of the big accounting firms. It would be a way I could work and get further schooling. Move up the ladder as they say."

Sarah felt her time for stalling was coming to an end. *Keep it together, Sarah. This will be hard on you both.*

CHAPTER ELEVEN

Mark and Heather got up and headed for the theater's exit. He was surprised by the movie. It was really a fun film. The mushy ending was entirely predictable, but up to that point it was a very enjoyable movie. He chuckled.

Heather noticed. Smiling, she asked "What?"

Mark smiled and said, "That bar scene. Where her spirit jumps into his body and they both fight over him trying to have a drink. That was hilarious!"

They both laughed at the memory.

Heather added, "You know, it's so easy to get lost in the story. You can overlook that Mark Ruffalo did all of it himself. It was such a great job of acting."

Mark nodded, "Yep, it was totally convincing. And, FUNNY."

Heather hooked her arm in Mark's and added, "Yes, it *was* terrific." They remained silent until they got to Mark's car. After they both got into the automobile, Mark started their drive back well below the speed limit.

"You know," said Heather, "you and Sarah share some of the same qualities."

"What do you mean?"

Heather looked at the speedometer and motioned with her head.

"All right, all right, don't tell me I drive like an old lady."

Heather feigned mock horror, "I would never refer to Sarah as an old lady."

Mark couldn't help but join Heather in laughter.

"Well, just so you know, I want to spend as much time with you as I can. So there." Heather hugged Mark's arm. She could have sworn the temperature inside the car was rising again.

* * *

Sarah continued as Mike Ahmadi was regaining his impatient demeanor.

"I found your father to be a very attractive man. He was sophisticated, different than anyone else I knew, at least personally, and so courteous and charming." Sarah realized the words were coming out of her mouth like a machine gun. She needed to calm herself down. She took a deep breath before she continued, "No one ever paid as much attention to me as he had. It was quite flattering and I felt myself, well, I guess smitten would be the right word."

Dear god, is this woman going to swoon over a memory she had of my father? So, he was young and ... What was the phrase? ... Oh yes, 'Sowing some wild oats'. I really don't want to hear about that.

Sarah could see Mike Ahmadi was pulling back. She knew what she had to say would be like a one-two punch but, she couldn't see any way to drag this out further. It was time for punch number one.

"Your father and I got closer and closer. Our relationship soon evolved into a physical one." Sarah needed to take another breath. She could see that the look on the young man's face had changed to a mixture of doubt and concern.

"Your father asked me if I was on birth control and ... I told him yes. Contraceptives are not accepted by the church and the only approved form of birth control was, and is, abstinence. I know nowadays many followers disavow this restriction but I ... just couldn't. I felt very guilty for lying to your father. But, when he found out I was pregnant, he was quite happy. I was very relieved. I thought everything would work out for us. I wouldn't have to reveal my deception."

Mike Ahmadi could see the woman was turning pale. He was starting to understand why she would have been important to his father. But why would she be distressed over such a happy memory unless something tragic happened? He had a sinking feeling he was going to hear something bad. He just hoped that it wouldn't cast a stain on his father's memory.

"When the school found out about my pregnancy, they put pressure on me to drop out. It became very hard to continue my studies. Your father let me stay with him in his apartment. I was close to running out of money, so he took over my expenses and paying for my prenatal care. Everything seemed fine. We were happy. Happy right up to the delivery of my baby boy."

Mike was shocked, "I have a half-brother? Where? WHERE?! I am the oldest son in my family, or I was. Please tell me!"

"It's not that simple," whimpered Sarah.

"What do you mean?!"

Sarah was now breaking down in tears. Mike realized he had raised his voice. This woman, despite whatever else she might be, had invited him to enter her home and also made him feel welcome. He thought, *Calm things down, asshole. You're shouting at an older woman. Your father would call your behavior shameful.*

Mike nodded to himself, "Ms. Bennington, I am very sorry I upset you. I think you can understand that everything you've told me is … a revelation."

"Yes, yes, I understand. It's difficult for us both."

Mike gave a small smile of sincerity, "Look, I won't be leaving to head back home right away and it's getting past the dinner hour. I'm staying at the hotel in the town of Antelope Valley. How would it be if I call you in the morning after you've had a night's rest and we can pick up with whatever remaining details you can share. Would that be all right with you?"

Sarah nodded, "So, I guess you've met Donnie then?"

Her comment made Mike grin, "Yes, the man has quite a mouth on him, doesn't he?"

Sarah smiled, "Yes, yes he does. Believe it or not, he's always been like that. I don't think there's any cure." She added, "If you wanted to stay for dinner, I would happy to fix something."

Mike immediately shook his head, "I absolutely could not inconvenience you any further. I would not be able to forgive myself. I promise I will call you tomorrow."

They both rose and walked to the front door.

Mike turned and said, "Ms. Bennington, I appreciate you taking the time to talk to me. I look forward to seeing you tomorrow."

Sarah gave a small smile and said, "I as well, Mr. Ahmadi, uh, sorry, Mike. I as well."

As Mike walked to his car, he thought, *I wonder if my half-brother is still alive? If he is, does she know where he is? I wonder what he looks like and what he does for a living. Does he have a family? I guess I will have to wait until tomorrow to find out.*

Sarah watched him get into his car, back out of her driveway and then disappear along the road he took to her house. *Little does he know the person he is thinking about will be staring at him tomorrow morning in his bathroom mirror.*

* * *

On the long slow drive home, Heather and Mark talked about a bunch of things. Where they both went to high school. What their favorite subjects were. What music each other liked. They had already agreed that there was at least one movie they both appreciated. No matter what it was, weather, sports, current events, they never seemed to run out things to talk about.

Heather said, "Okay, here's one. Favorite ice cream?"

Mark thought for a split second, "Cherry Garcia."

Heather laughed, "Almost as good as Chunky Monkey."

Mark faked being surprised, "Hey, that's my second most-favorite!"

Heather responded, "Okay, super serious now. What if there's no Ben & Jerry's … anywhere."

Mark shrugged, "Rocky Road."

Heather nodded, "R-o-c-k-y R-o-a-d." She shifted her hips to the right in the seat, took his right arm in hers and laid her left hand on his thigh. Mark wasn't sure what happened but it felt like his insides were ready to jump out. He was concerned she was leaving her hand there but also didn't want her to stop. It was quite a conundrum.

When they arrived at the farmhouse, they could see that the lights were off. Sarah didn't usually go to bed before 11 o'clock and when she did typically spent some time reading. Heather remembered she had said a visitor was there but no car was in the driveway other than Sarah's. She hoped everything was okay.

After parking the car, Mark got out and walked around to open the door for Heather.

"You don't need to see me to the door, I think I can find it," teased Heather.

"Ma'am, there's wild critters out here in these parts. Cain't be too careful."

That made Heather giggle. All Mark could think was, *How can this woman be cute and hot at the same time?*

When they arrived at the front door, Heather turned to face Mark. She had a serious look on her face. "Mark, I need to ask you something. You've spent so much time on me. Helping me, and it means the world to me but I can't help but wonder what you will get from this … relationship? I don't know if I can … if I know how … what I mean is … oh, hell, I don't know what I mean."

"Are you asking why I'm sticking by your side?"

"Well, that's an awkward way of putting it, but, yeah. I have no money. I'm starting my life over. I just don't understand what's in it for you."

Mark smiled, "Oh, the answer to that is simple."

"Really? So, what is it?"

Mark squeezed one eye shut and twisted his mouth slightly as he recalled a Sunday School lesson, "Again, the kingdom of heaven is like unto a merchant man, seeking goodly pearls: Who, when he had found one pearl of great price, went and sold all that he had, and bought it. Matthew 13, verses 45 and 46."

Heather cocked her head and said, "I don't get it."

Mark smiled, "Why, my dear Ms. Hollingsworth. You're my pearl of great price."

Heather jumped into his arms wrapping hers around his neck and kissing him so hard he thought he might chip a tooth. Once he felt the warmth of her body against his he thought, *Teeth be damned!*

When Heather and Mark managed to pry themselves apart, they moved over to the swing. They swung gently with their arms entwined and Heather resting her head on Mark's shoulder.

"I suppose you know that I'm falling for you."

"Heather, I fell off that cliff long ago."

"Really?"

"Really."

"So where do we go from here?"

Mark thought for a second then said, "Well, I guess we keep seeing a little bit more of each other and get closer and closer until we reach critical mass and explode."

Heather laughed out loud and then quickly

covered her mouth. Then she whispered, "I don't want to wake Sarah."

They got up and shared a long slow kiss and then Heather turned the doorknob to enter. Mark gave her a wink and whispered, "See you tomorrow?"

Heather nodded and mouthed *YES!*

When Heather entered the farmhouse, she saw that Sarah had left a note for her on the living room coffee table. It read:

> **Heather,**
>
> **I decided to retire a little earlier than usual. My company will be in town a little while longer and I'm planning on meeting them tomorrow at the hotel where they're staying. I need to ride in with you and use the car after dropping you off at the café. I'll make sure to get you home tomorrow. Please wake me if I'm not up when you start getting ready.**
>
> **Love, Sarah**

Heather chuckled to herself, *Well, I hope your visitor is used to Donnie's cussing and swearing.*

CHAPTER TWELVE

"Are you fuckin' kidding me!?" Deputy Martin Acosta was not particularly pleased to hear what Tom Burrton had to say.

"I know, I know, it sounds crazy as hell but that's what OSBI found. You'll need to decide on next steps." Tom knew Acosta would be aware that Tom would want to get out from under having to help untangle whatever circle-jerk happened that resulted in this situation.

"Antelope Valley … 200 and some miles away … you're sure." Martin phrased it as a question, but to Tom, the way he said it sounded like an indictment.

"That's what OSBI told me. The DNA from the head matches a hand and partial forearm that was found by Antelope Valley Police."

"Where exactly was that hand and arm found?"

"Martin, I don't know. You'll have to call the Antelope Valley Police Station for any further details."

"You know that this means I'll probably have

to get a facial reconstruction done."

"Yeah, I figured."

"Hope you're not expecting a raise this year. All right, well, thanks … for nothing, I guess."

"Sorry I couldn't help you out. Good Luck."

"Yep, I'm-m-m gonna need it."

Acosta disconnected the call. He reached over and pushed the power button on his computer then got up to go grab a cup of coffee. When he returned to his desk, his PC was ready to go. He started searching the department's directory for the phone number of the Antelope Valley Police Department, but then thought, *Awww, screw it. It's late. I'll start untangling this plate of spaghetti tomorrow.* Hitting the power once again to turn the device off, Acosta grabbed his coat and hat, started making his way to the front door bidding the regular goodbyes as he had done hundred's of times before. *At least I'll have a night's sleep and a hot cup of coffee before I have to start dealing with this pain in the ass.*

* * *

When he woke up the next morning, Acosta knew he had to make two phone calls – one to OSBI to get a recommendation for someone who could do forensic facial reconstruction and another to the Antelope Valley Police Station. Once he made it into the office, he had decided to switch the order and call the police station first to see if they could explain how the hell this craziness happened. It was odd that he was actually hoping it was a fuckup. It would, at least, be explainable.

Once he had retrieved a morning coffee and settled into his desk chair, he dialed the number for the Antelope Valley Police Station.

* * *

Mark Stoner brought his smile with him as he entered the police station the next morning. He had finished his morning run in record time. Completed his routine with weights, got ready and uncharacteristically arrived 10 minutes early. As he settled in at his desk, he thought, *I wonder if my smile will become permanent, not wearing off today ... or ... ever?* He was still smiling when the phone rang.

"Antelope Valley Police Station, Officer Mark

Stoner speaking."

"Hey. Martin Acosta here. I'm a deputy with the Creek County Sheriff's Department and … did you say your name was Mark Stoner?"

"Yeah, why?"

"Mark Stoner, former all-league fullback for Antelope Valley High?"

"Ye-a-a-h, back when quite a ways. Why are you asking about that?"

"Ha! I played for Bayer High School, middle linebacker. I was assigned to tackle you in the league championship game."

"That was you? You hurt my yards per carry average."

"Good to know. I just wish I could've done it without winding up on my back all night."

Stoner couldn't help but grin, "So what can I do for ya?"

"Well, I'm calling about a report from you guys regarding an arm and hand that was recovered but no body?"

Stoner nodded, "Yeah, yeah, that was a weird one."

"I need to speak to someone about the DNA result from that … specimen."

"The best person to talk to about that would be Sergeant Mike Glatt. He should be in at any time."

"Well, do you know where he found it?"

"Oh, he didn't find it, I did."

"Really. Where was it?"

"I found it in the middle of a farming field over in Berlin."

"Where the hell is that?"

Stoner described how one would drive there from Antelope Valley.

"That's over in Roger Mills County, why were you guys called?"

"Bad storm. Tornado damage. Lots of calls so we volunteered to help the Sheriff."

"Well, I'll be. You know …"

"Oh, hey Martin, Mike's walking in right now. How 'bout I let him take over?"

"Sure, that would be great. Thanks…but not for the bruises on my ass."

Stoner laughed, "You left a few on me too, buddy. Take care, I'm putting you on hold."

"Thanks."

Mark Stoner turned to look at Mike Glatt who had made a direct line to the break room for a cup of coffee and was now returning.

"Morning, Mike."

"Mornin'."

"I've got a Deputy Martin Acosta on the line. Wants to talk to you about an arm and hand."

Mike rolled his eyes, "This can't be good."

Stoner retorted, "Hey, you don't know that. Might bring some sunshine into your life. He's on line 2."

If Glatt's eyes could have rolled harder they would have ended up in the back of his skull, "What little fairy sprinkled pixie dust on you this morning?" Picking up the phone, he said, "Sergeant Glatt."

"Hello, Mike. This is Deputy Martin Acosta over in Creek County. I need to ask you a few questions about that body member you guys found, if you have a few minutes."

"How did you know my name was Mike?"

"Oh, had a little chat with Mark Stoner a minute or so ago."

"Well, did he fill you in on the where's and who's?"

"Pretty much. Said it was over in a place called Ber-LIN."

"Actually, they pronounce it BER-lin, even though it's spelled the same as the city in Germany."

"Okay, well, here's the thing. We located a head, badly damaged and no body, just the head."

Glatt could feel the hairs prickling up on the back of his neck, "Okay, go on."

"Well, it turns out, our DNA result is an exact match to the one you guys reported. Now, given that, you know, you're ..."

"200 miles away?"

"Y-e-a-a-h, roughly ... so, and don't take this personally, but any chance you guys screwed up somehow, contaminated specimen, improper procedure, or ...?"

"You know, normally that *would* be offensive. Ironically, I actually wish I could confirm that but I know the Medical Director of the Pathology Lab that did the test. It was over at Antelope Valley Medical Center. I'm also familiar with some of the staff there that do DNA testing. The Director is my uncle, so I can tell you he graduated in the top 5% of his medical school class. Those guys over there are top notch. I know that's not what you want to hear but it's a virtual certainty they did NOT screw up anything. On top of that, they duplicate any forensic testing just to make sure. What about on your end?"

"Tests were done by OSBI."

"Oh, they're a good group."

"Yeah, damn it, they are."

"So, other than accepting the impossible, what remains to be done?"

Acosta thought for a moment before answering, "I'm left with the only other option open to finding out who this is. Problem is, even though I'll get facial reconstruction done for the head, I don't know that there's anyone around here who would recognize it once it's completed. I'll have to advertise the photo all over the state. It's a headache … an expensive one."

Glatt leaned back in his chair and said, "Well, Martin, we might be able to fast track that bit for you."

"Oh? How?"

"Well, we are like 95% certain that the arm and hand belong to a guy named Roger Beaumont. It was found in the same vicinity as his car. A gun, .357 Magnum, which was found with the hand, was registered to Roger Beaumont. Problem we had in getting a death declaration was the lack of a body."

"So, this guy loses his head and flies it all over the state to land it in a field …"

Glatt completed the sentence, "200 miles away."

Acosta sighed, "I don't see how any of that helps."

Glatt answered, "His ex-wife is living in the area. If you can do a reconstruction that looks anything like him, she'll be sure to recognize it."

Mark Stoner had been listening in on Glatt's side of the conversation. When Heather was referenced, his head popped up. He didn't bother listening to Glatt's promise to help out when Acosta had more information. All he could do was ask himself what Heather's reaction might be upon seeing her dead husband's face. *Ex-husband*, he reminded himself. *I hope Roger Beaumont's ghost doesn't screw things up between me and Heather.*

CHAPTER THIRTEEN

When Sara had left the note and gone to bed, she couldn't asleep. She had continued pondering how, and how much of the past, to share with Mike Ahmadi - the man who was born Joseph Muhammad Nabul. That memory, long ago buried in a shallow grave, it seemed, was to arise and live once again.

*   *   *

She had come home to the apartment she shared with Muhammad Nabul. He had wanted to give his name to his son but Sarah had insisted on her Granddad's name, Joseph. So, the compromise resulted in little Joseph Muhammad Nabul having a name that, like himself, came from two different worlds.

Sarah had been at a mid-afternoon seminar and expected to come home, put away her book bag, kiss little Joseph on the forehead and greet her soon to be husband. When she arrived, she found the apartment dark and quiet.

"Hello? Muhammad? Hello?"

Sarah turned on the hanging ceiling light in the small dining area and sat her bag on the table. She paused to listen … straining to hear any sound. It was eerily quiet. When she turned, she saw the envelope taped to the front of the refrigerator in the kitchen. Just one word was written on the front, SARAH.

With hands shaking she took the envelope over to the dining table, pulled out a chair and sat down. She stared at the envelope. *Why did he use an envelope? He always leaves a note on the table when he takes our son for a walk in his stroller.* She stared at the envelope in her hands for several moments. Finally, she opened it. It read,

> Sarah,
> I know you will never be able to forgive me but I will not be able to forgive myself if I let my son grow up without the people and culture of my country. If you choose to join us in Afghanistan, you will not be accepted as a Christian and it will be hard for a non-Afghani, such as yourself, despite your adeptness in learning our language and religion. Nevertheless, you will be welcome in my house, My son and I will not be returning to America. I wish you happiness. By the time you read this, we will already be on our way.
> -Muhammad
> P.S.: The rent on the apartment has been paid for the next three months.

She ran to the bedroom and saw, with the exception of the crib, all of the baby's things - clothes, binky blanket, pacifier, stroller, everything had been taken. Sarah's scream as she wadded up the note could be heard throughout the apartment building. She returned to the chair sobbing, dropping the note as she sat down. It seemed her tears would never stop. Her life had been carved out leaving a hollow emptiness. Time stood still. Sometime later, loud voices and pounding on her door unfroze her from the chair.

"Police, open up! … Police!"

Sarah somehow made her way to the door. Opening it, she faced two police officers. The two police officers saw a young woman with red eyes and a tear-stained face. She looked to be in shock.

"Is everything all right here, ma'am?" asked the officer with two stripes on his sleeve.

Sarah opened her mouth to speak but no words would come out. The second officer stepped past Sarah and walked into the one-bedroom apartment. Walking through the kitchen, dining area, bathroom and finally the bedroom, he noticed the empty crib. There was nothing else in the room to indicate an infant had been there.

"Steve," said the other officer, "maybe we should bring her along to the station."

"Why, what did you find?"

Looking at Sarah's blank expression, he whispered into the officer's ear, "It's what I didn't find. Empty crib. Nothing else. Looks suspicious."

Officer Steve nodded, "Okay, Miss …?" There was still no response from Sarah. "All right, Miss, we are going to take you down to the station.

We'll get you settled and maybe then you can tell what went on here. Okay?" The words might as well have been jibberish. Sarah just moved along in a stupor as the officer guided her by the arm.

The other officer said, "Wait, I think I saw her bag on the table. She might need it."

Officer Steve waited in the hall with Sarah. The second officer returned with the bag and the wadded up envelope he discovered on the floor. When Sarah saw the envelope, she whimpered and then fainted.

*   *   *

When Sarah came to, she found herself in a padded holding cell. She had a terrible headache. While she had been unconscious, the police officers carried her past looky-loos to the patrol cruiser and transported her to the station. After reading the note in the envelope, they placed both items into an evidence bag and Sarah in the protective environment. Her bag contained identification along with her student ID. Her status as a student at the school meant she had health insurance, including counseling.

The psychologist who was called, briefly interviewed the officers about the circumstances in which they found Sarah. He advised them that he would evaluate her at the station if they had a suitable place to manage suicide watch and prevent her from possibly harming herself before he arrived. He told the officers, given what they said about her, that it would be best to not have her find herself in a mental health ward. If it came to that he would handle the intake order and they could move her from the station.

"Hello, Sarah." Said the man in the dark slacks and plaid coat. His off-white shirt was complemented with a navy-blue dickey.

I didn't know anyone wore those any more. "Who are you and how do you know my name?"

"I was contacted by the police here and given your name. Mine is Dr. Jim Kollath. but you can call me Dr. Jim or just Jim. Your choice."

'How about leave me alone?"

"Well, if that's what you want but don't expect me to answer to that right away."

"Are you really trying to be funny right now?

"God! My head hurts."

"Let me get you some aspirin and have them move you out of there. Do you want some water or coffee?"

"Hot tea."

"Okay, hot tea it is. I'll be right back"

Dr. Jim came back a few minutes later along with a police officer. The doctor waited with the aspirin and disposable hot-drink cup of tea while the officer unlocked the cell.

"Sarah, let's go down to Interview Room One. I have your aspirin and hot tea."

"Thank you." Sarah knew this guy was trying to help but it took all her strength to refrain from yelling at him. *Aspirin and hot tea are not a solution, I WANT MY SON!*

After entering the room, they sat down opposite from one another. Sarah took the aspirin that was offered as well as the cup of hot tea.

Dr. Jim said, "Wait, you might burn your mouth taking aspirin with that hot tea. Just a sec'."

Sarah watched him walk out of the room and through the cheap venetian blinds, stop at a drinking fountain, pull down a paper cup from the nearby dispenser and then proceed to fill it. Jim returned to the room, handed the cup of water to Sarah and returned to his chair.

"There you go."

"Thanks."

Sarah took the aspirin with the offered water and, realizing she was really thirsty, proceeded to drink all of it. She sat the empty cup down and then started sipping on the tea. Once her thirst had abated, she asked,

"Why was I locked in a cell? I didn't do anything."

Dr. Jim gave a slight smile, "That was strictly for your own protection. When the officers read the note they found, I advised them it would be a prudent thing to do."

"They read the note?!"

"Given the circumstances surrounding how they found you? Of course, they read it."

"So, they filled you in."

"Yes, to the extent that they could."

"Okay, how do I get my son back?"

"That you will need to take up with missing persons."

"So, why are YOU here?"

"I'm here to help you, Sarah."

"I don't need your help. I NEED MY SON!"

Sarah had almost risen from the chair when she realized that she was almost shouting. She slowly lowered herself.

"Sarah, everything that can be done to locate and return your son is being done. You've been through a very traumatic experience. Let's make sure you're in a good space mentally. For your son. Now, your insurance provides up to two weeks' worth of sessions. Why not make use of that benefit?"

It sounded like bull-crap to Sarah but she also knew that, if she had to fight Muhammad for custody, it would help to get a 'bill of health' from this psychologist.

"Okay," was all Sarah said in reply.

"All right, let's get you out to the Sergeant's desk. He wants to get some information from you about your son and your husband."

"He is ... *was* my fiancée. We were planning

on getting married in three months." Tears started to roll down her cheeks. Dr. Jim came around the table and taking Sarah gently by the arm said, "Let's get you over to the Sergeant." Sarah nodded.

It took about twenty minutes for Sarah to be interviewed. No promises were made, just that every effort would be expended. The FBI would be investigating since it involved international child abduction. They would also notify The Office of Children's Issues at the U.S. Department of State. As Sarah got up to leave, the Sergeant said, "Oh, here, before he left, Dr. Kollath said to make sure you have this card."

Sarah looked at the business card with the appointment date on one half and the time on the other. *Next Thursday at 2:30pm. The part of my life that isn't empty is a waste of time.*

Officer Steve walked up to the Sergeant as they both watched Sarah walk out of the police station, "Do you think she'll ever get her kid back?"

"Not a snowball's chance in hell."

CHAPTER FOURTEEN

The soft laughter brought Sarah back momentarily to the present. She looked at the clock face on the radio. Even after 2 hours, sleep eluded her. Heather's laughter made her glad that the sweet, young woman had found someone she could rely on. That part of this thing called life was good. The brief smile that crossed her lips was quickly erased by the return of memories that refused to die.

* * *

After leaving the police station, Sarah looked at the card again and tore it in two. She stopped at the trash can next to the entrance sidewalk but hesitated in throwing the pieces away. For reasons she wasn't quite sure of, she put the two pieces of the business card in her pocket.

Officer Steve had been watching the woman as she left. He couldn't imagine what she had been through. He had no children of his own but did have nieces and nephews. If anyone had taken one of them, he wouldn't rest until he got them back. He pushed through the front door and called to her,

"Excuse me. … Sarah?"

Sarah turned to see the approaching officer.

"Yes?" Sarah closed her right eye as she touched her temple. The headache had lessened but was stubbornly still there.

"Do you need a ride? It's no problem."

She started to say no but realized she was too far from the apartment to walk. Besides, she didn't feel well. So instead, she said,

"Well … yes. That would be very helpful."

The officer pointed at the cruiser they would be taking. After putting on seatbelts and getting underway an awkward silence ensued.

"I'm sorry about your situation. I really …"

"I don't want to talk about it."

"Okay … sorry." After a pause, Officer Steve cleared his throat. "I do want to say one thing, and please hear me out, then I'll shut up."

Sarah sighed, closed her eyes and nodded.

"Take Jim Kollath's advice and see him. He helped me through some … tough stuff. It won't be a waste of your time."

Sarah opened her eyes and turned to look at

the officer. He appeared to be sincere. She felt in her pocket and touched the torn pieces of the business card. *Maybe one visit couldn't hurt. All I have right now is loss and loneliness.*

After they had arrived at her apartment, Sarah got out of the cruiser, mumbled a 'thank you' and turned to face the building. It felt like her feet were made of lead. Her world had been full of love and promise. Now what was left was a ragged, gaping hole of sad emptiness.

CHAPTER FIFTEEN

Martin Acosta was still chuckling over his conversation with Mark Stoner when he dialed Tom Burrton's extension. *Boy, that guy was noooo fun to tackle.*

"Forensics lab, Burrton speaking."

"Oh, hey Tom, it's Martin. Say, do you have someone over at OSBI that can direct me on how to get a facial rec' done?"

"Hm, yeah, I'm pretty sure Nadene can help out. It's not her area but she's a sharp cookie, she'll know someone for you to contact."

"Great, can you give me her number?"

"Sure, are you ready?"

"Shoot."

Acosta wrote the number on his desk pad, he would transfer it to his phone contacts later. He repeated the number back to Tom just to confirm.

"That's it."

"Okay, Tom, thanks."

"Good luck."

Acosta disconnected the call and punched in the number on his multi-line desk phone.

"OSBI, can I help you?"

"Is this Nadene Honeycutt?"

"Yes, may I ask who's calling?"

"Yeah, this is Martin Acosta, I'm with the Sheriff's Department over in Creek County."

"Is this about that … head?"

Martin's eyebrows raised, "Yes, yes, it is. How did you know that?"

"Tom had sort of given me a *heads* up. Besides that, with the circumstances being what they are, the only reason you would be calling is to figure out how to confirm an identity. Otherwise, you wouldn't be contacting us over here."

Overlooking the terrible pun, Acosta answered, "Yeah, it looks like we need to do a facial recognition build on the head we found. The only good news is we have a lead on someone who might be able to do an identification once that's completed. Do you know who I should contact?"

"Yeah, Pete Wolfe. He's been involved in some new stuff in that regard. I even heard he's been looking for, lack of a better word, specimens. Apparently, he got a grant of some sort. It would be worth your time to check with him first. If it doesn't work out, let me know. There's a gal over at OU that does sculpting and if I'm remembering correctly, she's done a few of these in the past."

"Okay, do you have those phone numbers handy?"

"I have the department number. Just call and ask for Pete. I forgot the name of the gal over at OU but I have that department number as well. Here they are."

Acosta took down the information, "All right, Nadene, thanks a lot."

"No problem. Anything else, just give me buzz."

Before he could respond, he heard the call disconnect.

"Busy gal," muttered Acosta.

Acosta once again dialed a number he hoped would lead to some answers on this bizarre case. He heard the ringing. It rang twice. Just before the third he heard,

"Yeah?"

"Um, I need to speak to Pete, this is …"

Before Acosta could continue he heard a voice away from the phone yelling,

"Hey, Pete! Guy on the phone for ya!" After a moment's pause, the male voice continued, "He's comin'."

"Tha …" Once again, before he could finish the word, he could tell the phone had already been laid down. After what was two minutes that seemed like twenty, he heard,

"Pete Wolfe."

"Oh, yeah, Pete, this is Deputy Martin Acosta over at the Creek County Sheriff's Department."

"Okay."

Well, apparently not everyone has heard about my head dilemma. "I've got a situation where I need a facial recognition done and I hear you're the guy to talk to about it."

"Well, yeah, we are doing that here but, if it's just a cranial build, you can get that done over at OU. Myra Young can help you out."

"I'm not sure if the Medical Examiner will be willing to strip off all the flesh on the head we have."

"Are you saying the head is fresh and you

need a facial reconstruction done?"

"Yeah, it's been really badly beaten up, maybe gnawed on by wild animals and the skull has a few of what look like claw marks on it. Half the face is gone and pretty much both eyes. It's …"

Wolfe interrupted, "Are any pieces of the skull missing?"

Acosta thought for a moment, "No, no, I don't think so. There are some claw marks on the forehead as I mentioned. Basically, you could say it's half defleshed."

"That's exactly what I've been looking for."

"Really?"

"Yeah, I've gotten a grant to use CAT scan and computer modeling to generate facial reconstruction in 3-D. It's important we include challenging, umm, *samples* in the grant study to show just how well this can work. It's going to be a cheaper, quicker and more reliable method than the old sculpting process."

"Just out of curiosity, what if the witness is blind and can only tell by touch?"

Wolfe had a 3-word reply, "3-D Printer."

"Wow. Okay, what's next?"

"I'll email you a submission form. Get it signed off by whomever on your end and as soon as I get it back, .pdf by email is fine, I'll make arrangements for the transfer of, uh, your … head. You know what I mean."

Acosta laughed, "Yeah, yeah, I got it. Thanks, I'll get right on that. Let me give you my email."

CHAPTER SIXTEEN

Sarah's sleepless musing of her past still paraded through her brain like scenes from a movie, a Horror movie she decided..

She had dropped her classes the following day after getting back to her empty apartment. She spent her time between being doubled over with ache and misery and crying her eyes out. She hardly ate anything. She had gone back and forth about seeing that guy, Jim Kollath. She looked yet again at the two pieces of his business card. She still hadn't decided whether to go or not. The first appointment would be the next day. *I'll decide tomorrow,* she thought to herself.

Tomorrow came and she still hadn't made up her mind. All through the mechanical brushing of her teeth, showering, getting dressed and brushing of her hair she still hadn't made a decision one way or the other. Finally, she told herself,

"Okay, if it's sunny out, I'll go. If it isn't sunny, I'll blow this guy off."

Sarah knew the weather report had predicted rain, so she fully expected to see nothing but clouds as she opened the apartment's venetian blinds. The sunlight streaming in was so strong that it made her eyes water. She sighed, "Well, shit."

* * *

She recalled that first visit to Dr. Kollath. He welcomed her warmly and had her sit on a sofa while he took an off-angled chair next to the coffee table they both shared. There was a steaming cup of tea on a coaster in front of the place she was sitting. He crossed his legs, opened a writing portfolio and took out a pen. He motioned to the cup on the coffee table.

"Just in case you would like something to sip. Don't feel obligated to drink it if you don't want."

Sarah simply nodded.

"Sarah, what we're going to work on with our sessions is finding a way for you to work through your grief and setting a strategy for you move forward. A new beginning of sorts."

"What are you talking about? I need to get my son back. That's the only thing that matters."

"Are you sleeping through the night? Have you regained your appetite? Are you eating regularly?"

This guy is making me nervous. Is he a mind reader?

Sarah couldn't bring herself to respond. Apparently, she didn't need to.

"What you are experiencing isn't unique to you. Others have had to deal with loss as well. You aren't alone. We'll work through the grieving process together."

"How does this help get my son back?"

"By making sure that his mother is strong physically and mentally."

Sarah couldn't figure out an argument so she acquiesced. She had misunderstood what Dr. Kollath meant at the time they first met by 'two weeks' of sessions. She had naively thought that it meant 14 sessions daily in a row. It was a bit of a shock when he mentioned the sessions were weekly. *This is going to last three months!*

To Sarah it seemed the meetings with Jim, he insisted on using his first name, were tediously long. In each session, they decided on an objective for the week. She would take up walking the first week for twenty minutes a day. It would go up to thirty minutes the following week and so forth. Her appetite started to return. By the time she was walking a solid hour a day, the session times seemed to shrink. When he would tell her that their time was up, she would feel a tinge of disappointment.

He had recommended a counseling group; talking with other women who had experienced loss, finding a way to express her grief in words and knowing that she was being heard by people who truly understood her pain.

Eventually, he started guiding her toward thinking about herself differently. She had encapsulated herself as a wife and mother. He suggested that she adopt a new outlook; sort of a 'vision of what she was *going* to be'. He explained that she would always be a mother but she was also more than that. She could make a life moving forward being someone new, not so much as to forget the past but not letting it dictate her future.

The frequency of her phone calls to the FBI and US State Department were so frequent during this time they would put her on hold for twenty minutes or longer in hopes she would hang-up or stop calling.

It was this rudeness that helped her focus on her next move. She was also helped by the oddest little thing. Jim Kollath had given her a card during one of her last sessions. It was almost oxymoronic but it somehow made an impression on her as Jim said it did on him. It read,

---

Life is what it is...

Accept it,
And deal with it the very
best you can.

Keith Golay, PhD

When Sarah first saw it, she thought, *How silly is this?* Jim had told her that he thought the same thing when he first saw it but, at the time, he had just finished reading a book by Eckhart Tolle. The main theme of the book was living in the present. He had asked his therapist, Keith Golay, if he could have a bunch of them to hand out. Sarah kept hers in her purse everyday from then on and lost track of the number of times she had looked at it. It too helped her figure out her next move. She would apply to work at the State Department. If she couldn't get their assistance from the outside, maybe doing it from the inside would be more successful.

* * *

The three months of sessions had gone by much more quickly than Sarah had anticipated. She had managed to get a paid internship at the U.S. State Department and was anxious to share the good news with Jim Kollath. She would finally be on a path, with some luck, to finding her son. *And, getting him back!*, She told herself.

When she arrived for her final scheduled appointment she knocked and, upon hearing the now familiar voice say, "Come in", entered the room to find a steaming cup of tea sitting on the coffee table. It had become part of the ritual for these sessions. She took her usual position on the couch and Jim, his in the chair. He took his notepad and pen in hand and looked at Sarah.

"You seem a little fidgety today. Is everything all right?"

Sarah smiled and said excitedly, "I've gotten a

paid internship and I start on Monday!"

Jim Kollath smiled back, "How wonderful. You're putting yourself out there. That is very positive news Sarah. What will you be doing if I might ask?"

Sarah's smile faded a little, "Well, I'm not sure exactly, it's a combination of work and study. It's meant to be a way of entering a career. But, that's not the important part."

Kollath crossed his hands on top of the notepad, "Oh? Really? What is the important part?"

Sarah's smile grew once again, "I'll be working in the U.S. State Department. See?" She stopped to take a sip of tea.

Kollath was growing concerned, "I'm not sure. Do you mind explaining it to me?"

Sarah cocked her head slightly when she looked at Kollath, *How can he not get it?*, "I'll be working inside the State Department? I'll have an inside track on finding my son?"

Kollath now was concerned, "Sarah, I'm concerned."

Sarah frowned, "Concerned? Why?"

"Even though it's apparent you've made good progress, don't you think you're pushing yourself too hard, expecting too much of yourself?"

"What? That's silly. I've gone through all of the sessions. Of course I'm ready to move on."

"Sarah, these sessions were just those that your insurance covered. Therapy is a process of change and evaluation. It can't be limited to checking off boxes on a calendar. In fact, I was going to discuss future sessions with you today since this is the last one we had scheduled so far."

"You thought I was going to need…to want…to…acquiesce to more of these?!"

"Well, yes, there is more to be done. More to be worked through."

Sarah stiffened, "More to work through? How can you say that? I've come to each and every one of these. I've gotten back to my normal weight. I'm exercising every day." She paused for a moment and then added, "And, I've gotten a new job. How could you possibly think there is more to do?"

"What job did you get and why?"

Why is Jim acting like a knucklehead?

Shaking her head, Sarah said, "I've already told you!"

"Do you see why I might find that concerning?"

"No, no I do not. What are you trying to pull?"

"Nothing, I'm just pointing out tha …"

"Pointing out nothing! I'm done and I'm moving on. You said those words when we first met and by God that's what I'm doing. I appreciate your help but it's not needed anymore. Goodbye, Dr. Kollath."

With that declaration, Sarah got up and left the office, closing the door behind her.

Jim Kollath said, "Goodbye, Sarah, be well." The words were blunted against a closed door.

Looking at this notepad and sighing, Jim Kollath turned over a fresh sheet, clicked his ballpoint pen and wrote in capital letters, UNRESOLVED. After tearing off the sheet and wadding it up, he tossed it into the open wastebasket beside his desk. He mused,

"Well, at least I scored at *something* today."

He hoped against it, yet knew, that Sarah was setting herself up for a relapse. *Maybe it will never happen,* he lied to himself.

CHAPTER SEVENTEEN

Sarah had applied through what was called a PathWays Program. It was not technically an internship. It was a one-year program that was supposed to lead to a career-path decision. She figured that one year would be all she'd need to locate her son and arrange, somehow, to get him returned home to America. The State Department offered five areas of service; Consular, Economic, Management, Political and Public Diplomacy. The intent was to have applicants choose a career path from among them depending on their interests and willingness to meet the '13 DIMENSIONS' that reflect the 'skills, abilities, and personal qualities deemed essential to the work of the Foreign Service at the United States Department of State.' Once you had done all this, you would be a highly skilled and terribly underpaid Foreign Service Officer.

Sarah smiled ruefully as she recalled her decision to work in the Consular branch. After all, it should be a shoo-in to get assigned to Afghanistan, right?

She was assigned to assist in dealing with the

Mexican Embassy. At the time she knew very little Spanish but there wasn't much pressure to be fluent as her primary job was basically as a paper pusher.

The time wasn't a total waste. She did gain fluency in Spanish and also learned that the Consular track was NOT where she wanted to be. She wanted to interact with people, particularly those that had political pull. Those that could help locate and, God willing, assist in retrieving her son. She had burned up two years, one in the Pathways program and another with the Mexican consulate and was well into the third when she somehow managed to get moved over to the Political track. It had almost been like starting over. She even had to get coffee for senior officers and she had almost been assigned to Uganda.

She rolled her eyes thinking about what it would be like to interact with a leader whose 'spiritual/religious movement ' which manifested as an armed rebel group. The leader, one Alice Lakwena directed actions at the behest of the spirits who possessed her. The story was that Alice was directed to form the group, known as HSM (Holy Spirit Movement), by one of her spirits; Lakwena. It was no wonder the region remained in constant turmoil.

The irony of how someone could be so dedicated to a futile pursuit was lost on Sarah. African countries were interesting to her but they were not at the center of her goal. She had only one mission in her life, the retrieval of her son and she was going to pursue it come hell or high water.

She kept up on any news that came out of Afghanistan, which was minimal. One day it was announced that Russia had formally exited Afghanistan but the vacuum had been filled by the Taliban. Pakistan wanted Afghanistan to be an Islamic state rather than a nationalist one. Pakistan's geographic and political importance meant pressure from Washington had to not only be applied judiciously but also gently. Over the ensuing years indications were that the Taliban would not be content with anything other than total and complete control of Afghanistan.

Afghanistan is a diverse country made up of different ethnicities and languages. The unifying factor is religion. Almost all of the inhabitants are Muslim; the large majority being Sunni, the minority (numbering over two million and mainly Hazaras), Shiite. The language spoken most frequently in the peripheral provinces is Dari. However, the most common language in the central portion of the country is Pashto.

Sarah had made it a habit of using an Afghani lullaby to keep up on her Pashto pronunciation. It was a lullaby that Muhammad had taught her after she overheard him singing it to little Joseph. It helped to keep at least rudimentary skills in the language and act as a reaffirmation of her purpose.

Now that the Taliban had made their intentions clear, the State Department as well as the CIA were very interested in maintaining a watch, and an ear, on any activity occurring in that country. Both agencies were grabbing anyone they could find that spoke either Farsi, Dari or especially Pashto. It was during a a rest break to brew some tea in the break room and once again beginning her lullaby in a soft voice that she was overheard.

Don Smith was a liaison from the CIA to the State Department. Mark Samm was running lead for the State Department for Afghanistan affairs. They were talking animatedly as they walked by the open door to the break room.

"Mark, are you sure there's no one else?"

"Don, you've already commandeered more people than I had available for this."

Don sighed, "I think the Taliban are planning a move in the north. We just don't know when or if it's an offensive or leverage to force negotiations."

"Well, I can't help …"

"Wait, … what's that? Hear that?"

They both had passed the open doorway of the break room and now stood watching a woman bounce a tea bag up and down in her cup while singing softly … IN PASHTO!

Mark Samm was the first to speak, "Excuse me, Ms. Bennington, I believe it is?"

Sarah turned to see two men staring at her. Because of her surreptitious inquiries, she was aware of who Samm was. She didn't want to give anything away by appearing too familiar.

"Yes," replied Sarah, "and you are?"

"My name, is Mark Samm and this is Don Smith. I'm tasked with keeping an eye on

Afghanistan." Upon hearing this, Sarah's heart rate accelerated.

"Okay. And … what do you do, Mr. Smith?"

"I work for the government."

Sarah nodded. She had an idea as to which agency he did 'government work' for.

"Gentlemen, how can I help you?"

Mark gestured to a table with three chairs, "Can we sit?"

Sarah shrugged, moved to set her tea on the table and, before she could move her chair, Mr. Smith pulled it out for her. It didn't feel like a gallant gesture.

Mark continued, "We think things are heating up in Northern Afghanistan. We have a number of monitoring channels but not enough people who speak Pashto to man them. Dari, yes, but Pashto no. Would you be interested in joining our team?"

Sarah leaned back, "Well, my Pashto is a little rusty and …"

Don Smith interrupted, "You'll have a resource fluent in Pashto to back you up for anything that you don't understand. But, our problem, as Mark indicated, is that he's our only expert. You could look at this as an opportunity to help your country and brush up on your Pashto."

Sarah smiled slightly but didn't find his humor amusing. She did see, though, an opportunity. It had taken twelve years to get to this point and now, just as she was on the cusp of giving up, out of the blue an opportunity for a position that might help find her son. She had yelled, cursed and screamed at God so many times for what had happened but no explanation was received, no matter how hard she listened. Now, a path might have been provided, IF SHE WAS CAREFUL.

* * *

The new position placed Sarah at PAF Camp Badaber, Pakistan. She worked in a monitoring room located in a nondescript building within the complex. There were a half dozen listening stations set up within the room, all within earshot of each other. She along with the other analysts, were tasked with preparing daily transcripts of monitored radio traffic. It was tedious work listening to everything from road work arguments being bandied about and, on occasion, aircraft traffic taxiing a runway.

She feared this job would also end up being a dead end and just when she felt like she was getting close. Then, one fateful day, she overheard one of the other Foreign Language Analysts, Samuel, pose a question to two nearby colleagues.

"Have either of you heard of a guy named Muhammad Nabul? His name is coming up with some communications regarding Mazir-i-Sharif." The two analysts shook their heads.

Sarah's ears perked and her heart started pounding. *Should I say something? How do I play this? Will I be kicked off the team due to a personal conflict or would it be considered a benefit?* She decided to keep her cards close to her chest.

"I think I've come across that name before," offered Sarah.

"Oh, in what context?"

"None, really, just in passing. Don't know why it stuck. What have you heard?" asked Sarah.

"Someone referred to him as Mayor and asking what they should do with the soldiers." This was followed by a gesture meant to convey, *I don't know what it means.*

"Was there a battle of some kind?"

"Not that I know of but that doesn't mean anything. Do you want to sit in?"

Sarah did her best to shrug nonchalantly, "Sure, why not?"

"Okay, give me a sec to clear it with the supervisor."

Sarah nodded and mentally crossed her fingers. After an apparent brief conversation between Samuel and their supervisor in the small office at the opposing end of the room, the analyst reappeared in the doorway and motioned for Sarah to join them.

After sitting down, the supervisor asked Sarah, "So how do you know this … what's his name?"

Samuel responded, "Muhammad Nabul."

"Okay, this Muhammad Nabul?"

Sarah cleared her throat, "Well, sir, after hearing it again, I just remembered that I had taken a couple of classes with a Muhammad Nabul back at Georgetown."

The supervisor paused then said, "All right, do

you think you could recognize his voice if this is the same Muhammad Nabul?"

Sarah squirmed in the chair, "Well, I might be able..."

"Okay, sit in with Samuel here. We'll give it a week. If it appears that it's the same guy, maybe that'll help us figure out what those conversations are about."

Sarah nodded and stood. She and Samuel left the office and walked directly to the listening stations. Samuel jacked a headset for her and they both started the laborious task of waiting for something meaningful.

After three days that felt like three weeks, Sarah heard a voice that gave her a start. It was Muhammad. Samuel noticed her jerky movement.

"You remember this guy's voice don't you." It was not phrased as a question but she took it as one. Sarah nodded then answered deceptively.

"Yes, I'm surprised that I still recognize it."

"What do you remember about him? Is he honest, devious, untrustworthy, a solid citizen, what?"

Sarah paused a moment then said, "Well, he

definitely struck me as capable of subterfuge but he also seemed to be a decent person." She followed this with a shrug that she hoped contained a 'don't know much more than that' connotation.

"Well, I think we need to tell the supervisor your stint needs to be more than one week."

"I agree."

CHAPTER EIGHTEEN

Information as well as misinformation continued to trickle out of Iraq and even though it appeared that something major had occurred at Mazir-i-Sharif, trying to separate fact from fiction became nearly impossible. Then, Sarah got a break she had hoped for but hadn't expected. Don Smith approached her a few days later.

"Sarah, we need you to go to our station in Peshawar."

"I'm sorry, I don't understand. That's only 15 kilometers or so north."

She wondered if she'd overplayed her hand. She felt that she should appear somewhat opposed to the idea before relenting.

"There are reports of refugees coming into Pakistan from Iraq and some of them are from Mazir-i-Sharif, and the majority are women and children. The women are tight-lipped around foreign men and the children, well, the children can't be trusted as reliable sources."

"I see."

"So, you being one of the few women we have

that are fluent in Pashto, it would really help to get an idea of what's going on. I've already cleared it with Mark."

She didn't trust that he actually had but it was putting her closer to the Afghanistan border. She had no actual plan other than make her way inch by inch.

"All right, when do I leave?"

"Tomorrow morning, oh-six-hundred. Take enough clothes and personal items to last you a week. After that, plan on coming back here for a debrief. A four-wheel off roader will be ready to take you from here. They're expecting you at Peshawar station."

* * *

She had seen folks down on their luck before but none of it had prepared Sarah for the devastation and loss that she saw in the eyes of the refugees she encountered at Peshawar.

Many of them only had the clothes on their backs and a number were injured. It was hard to tell if it was the result of conflict or the terrible toll of leaving one's homeland with nothing.

It took several days before Sarah was able to get anyone to open up about what had transpired.

Once she convinced them to share their stories, she immediately regretted it.

Apparently, what analysts had picked up on monitored airways were snippets regarding the successful push back against Taliban soldiers by the United Front, a coalition of forces fighting against Taliban control. Mazir-i-Sharif was the only major city where the United Front maintained control. Several thousand Taliban soldiers had been killed during the two-month assault.

The refugees who stayed several days following the next assault, presumably a retaliation for the killing of the soldiers, gave details of those final days. They reported that a Taliban general had made an agreement with the mayor of Mazir-i-Sharif, Muhammad Nabul, that if United Front soldiers removed themselves from the city, then the Taliban would not seek revenge. As soon as the UF soldiers vacated the city, the Taliban general's lie was unveiled. Taliban soldiers engaged in a massacre. Organized searches were conducted for men and boys who were Hazara, Tajik and Uzbek. During these searches dozens, perhaps hundreds of male Hazara were summarily executed. The killing was indiscriminate; among the civilian casualties were eight officials from the Iranian consulate. Even pets were shot.

It felt like a heavy stone pressing on Sarah's heart. She knew it meant that her only son and his father had been murdered. Just as she thought she was on the cusp of making contact, God had wiped away her future. The universe was collapsing in on her.

* * *

Sarah wasn't sure what her colleagues thought or said about her after her departure. The following two weeks were a blur in her memory. Barely conscious of her arrival back in DC, she refused to work, eat or, sleep in any consistent way. It had finally come down to being called in for an exit interview with Human Resources. She somehow summoned the strength to show up not quite understanding why she had bothered. Mark Samm was apparently aware of the exit interview. Unknown to her at the time, he called up the HR department manager. He hadn't understood why Bennington appeared to have broken down so dramatically.

When he had the manager on the line, he asked about Sarah.

"So, what's the story with Bennington?"

"Resigned."

"I *know* that. Did she explain what happened and why … you know."

"I wouldn't be able to share personal information of that nature, but, no. Just sat and cried."

"She didn't say *anything*?!"

"When I explained the process for her exit, she nodded that she understood, but no words were forthcoming."

"So we only know that it was something involving the refugees from Mazir-i-Sharif."

"If you say so."

"So, nothing else?"

"I could fax you a copy of the exit interview but there's no real information on it other than a few tear stains next to her signature."

Sighing, Mark Samm replied, "Don't bother. Well, I guess it's time to just move on. Hope she can find a way to do that as well."

"Yes, she appeared extremely depressed."

"Okay then, thanks … I guess. Goodbye."

Upon hearing the 'goodbye' returned, followed by a dial tone, Mark Samm replaced the handset onto the desk phone's resting place.

CHAPTER NINETEEN

Sarah contacted her friend back home to arrange things after her relocation to America. He wired some money so that she could get by for a couple of weeks. That was as far into the future as her mind would allow. She put off his questions about any of her future plans. She thought to herself, *What future?*

Sarah located a short-term rental at a place called *Apartment B*, primarily because it was within walking distance of Georgetown University. After a restless night, she went out for a walk mid-morning the next day and immediately felt that being here was a mistake. Mental pictures of little Joseph swirled around. Even Muhammad's face, as sad and furious as the man who abducted her son made her, floated by with that charming smile of his. The ache that had mostly subsided started intensifying again. She tried to distract herself by walking toward the university.

The campus came into view and it was like seeing an old friend after a long absence. The memory of classes, some terribly hard, some so interesting she almost lost herself in the subject, came close to making her smile, but the empty sadness - the burden of loss, intruded over and over again.

She found herself in front of the Dahlgren Chapel of the Sacred Heart. The red brick building with its high arched doorway, nestled amongst buildings with two large trees standing guard to either side almost glowed under the direct sunshine bathing its steeple. Anger and need fought inside her as the structure beckoned for her to enter. Anger won.

"Not on your life," she said out loud but quietly. "Not after you allowed my son to be taken from me and then killed." The tears, once again, started trickling down her cheeks. She sat down on the middle rung of the semi-circled steps, guarded silently by two rotund pedestals.

She continued to mutter, "Why is this still happening? Why has savage violence followed me throughout my life? And why to those I cherish and love? Could I, SHOULD I, have done anything differently? Am I the reason all this has happened? Why didn't God DO something?! Maybe I AM the reason. If I do something about me, maybe that will prevent any more harm to others." She momentarily pondered suicide. Sarah hadn't taken notice of the woman who approached.

Sister Mary Theresa had attended a lecture at Gaston Hall and, being new to Georgetown and the surrounding area, wanted to visit the chapel before returning to Boston. As she approached she momentarily halted when she noticed the woman on the steps who appeared to be struggling with something, at least to the point of talking to herself. It occurred to her that the woman might be mentally ill but, seeing that she was well dressed and not elevating her voice, decided to make contact. She hoped that her brown leather flats would serve as decent enough running shoes if she needed to escape.

"Hello, there," she said softly, "do you mind if I join you?"

Sarah was startled by the sudden interruption, "Oh, um, well, yeah, it's a free country." Sarah wiped both cheeks with the back of her hand. Sarah watched as the middle-aged woman in the soft beige sweater with an overlaid white collar, smoothed her plaid skirt and sat down an arms-length from Sarah. The woman clasped her hands around her knees.

Nothing was said between the two women for several moments. Sister Mary Theresa decided to speak up, "I'm visiting the area. I attended a seminar at Gaston Hall on the Georgetown campus and wanted to see Dahlgren before I go back home."

Sarah gave a slight nod.

Mary Theresa continued, "Are you from this area?"

"Used to be." *Good god, leave me alone.*

"Well, um, if you have any advice for a newbie like me as to what to look at before the day after tomorrow, please tell me. I would really appreciate it."

"The only thing here is heartache and misery."

"Oh, I'm so sorry to hear that." After a pause, she added, "Perhaps we should go inside. That might help."

"What? Ask God for something!?"

Mary Theresa was taken aback by the woman's emphatic response.

"Well, I'm suggesting prayer, actually, but it is okay to ask God for help."

Sarah snickered, "Hmph, not if you expect an

answer and *especially* not if you want your son returned to you."

Sarah immediately regretted letting so much personal information slip out. It had come out like a torrent, a flash flood and it seemed impossible to stop.

"No, no, God's answer is to let them be killed. So, I'm not asking a murderer for anything."

The woman remained calm. It really irritated Sarah. She had expected her to move back or leave but instead she leaned in and asked a crazy question.

"What's your name?"

Sarah hesitated slightly, being thrown a little off-balance, "Um, it's, uh, Sarah." She maintained enough caution to not let go of her last name.

"Hello, Sarah, nice to meet you. I'm Sister Theresa," she said as she held out her hand.

Sarah stared at the hand being offered and slowly moved hers into its grasp. "You don't look like any nun I've known."

Sister Theresa ignored the comment and, after the brief handshake, said,

"I can understand your feelings, Sarah, but God isn't the one to blame, and before you try to say it, neither are you."

Sarah was irate, "How can you say that!? You don't know anything about me! You don't know what it's like to lose a son only to find out that he and his father were killed!"

Sister Theresa faced forward and said, "I've lost two children to stillbirths and before we could try for a third pregnancy my husband was killed while serving in the Persian Gulf. He was on the USS Stark when it was struck by missiles from an Iraqi fighter jet. He died along with 36 other sailors."

Sarah's hand went to her mouth. She didn't know what to say. She wanted to ask this woman, this *Nun?,* how she had dealt with such loss. Sarah could see that the woman had shut her eyes and her lips were barely moving but Sarah couldn't make out any sound. *What? Is she praying?*

Sister Theresa mentally worked through the rosary beads she hadn't brought with her, *Holy Mary, Mother of God, Pray for us sinners now and at the hour of death.* After five quick repetitions, she calmed down and then began to admonish herself, *Mary Theresa, you know better. Your mission is to show*

mercy to the world, not push aside this woman's grief
by imposing your own.

She opened her eyes and looked at Sarah, "I'm sorry. I shouldn't have said anything and especially not burdened you with my grief in your time of need." Sarah just shook her head as if to say, *No, it's okay. I understand.*

The ice had been broken. The two women slowly opened up to each other. They discussed their experiences; the anger, the guilt, the sense of helplessness. After a little more than an hour of chatting, something Sister Theresa said made an impression on Sarah.

"I know this isn't within the theology of the church, Sarah, but I really believe it. Heaven and Hell aren't some imaginary places either 'up there' or 'down there'. I know deep in my soul that Heaven and Hell are within each of us. The decision we have to make is, where will we choose to reside?"

Sarah remembered it was at that moment she made the completely irrational decision to go with this woman to Boston.

* * *

She recalled that the time in Boston had been a time of healing. At first, if felt ironic to have spent so many months screaming at God to then end up working for him. Well, that is, if things worked out. The order she was going to be joining were the Sisters of Charity. Their motto was *Compassion, Forbearance, Forgiveness*. Even though she knew the meaning she looked up each word in a worn thesaurus she found in the library of Merciful Mother Cathedral. It probably should have come as no surprise that the word 'mercy' was a synonym for each word comprising the motto. It also seemed pre-ordained that she would want to take the religious name Mary Mercy. As a novitiate, she lobbied so hard for it that people started calling her by that moniker before she actually received it formally.

Everything seemed to progress normally until the disturbing rumors started circulating within the church. Sarah felt compelled to help young boys who appeared to be on their own. She found a like-souled individual to partner with her in finding adoptive homes. The fact that this occurred outside normal channels – her disingenuous term for 'illegal' was beside the point to her. However, it all ended with the encounter of a young teenage boy who spoke Pashto and was found sitting outside the office of Archbishop Hamlin. The repercussions from his unexpected absence had caused a brouhaha that not only affected her future but also the future of Sister Theresa. To this day, Sarah felt guilty that Mary Theresa was punished along with herself. The punishment, euphemistically referred to as 'reassignment', had the two women ending up at St. Ruth's Church in North Kansas City, Missouri.

* * *

The muffled sound of a cough from Heather brought Sarah back to the present. All she had mulled over, the phases of her life, the tragedy that drove her away from this farm. The tragedy that influenced her decision to leave grad-school, work at the State Department in order to chase after little Joseph. All the years wasted only to receive the news of her son's death, only now known to be false, nearly drove her to end it all. Her decision to join dear Mary Theresa in Boston had been a reprieve, but it was short-lived, resulting in them both being shipped away to Kansas

City. She had found a meaningful life at St. Ruth's but even that eventually turned tragic.

Sarah recalled the young drug criminal who had held her hostage and died mere moments later from a detective's bullet. She still remembered the feeling of his warm blood as it splattered across her face. Her friend Henry, the janitor, and his sister had to go into Witness Protection. It didn't matter that Sarah wasn't directly at fault. Violence followed her everywhere she went. Maybe, now that she was back at the family farm, she could find some peace. It was the only place where, for as long as she had lived there, no terrible things had happened. It seemed that her life had been spent running away only to have heartache and tragedy find her again and again. The nightmares had only recently begun their demise, most likely due to the presence of lovely young Heather.

She knew Heather would be waking soon. Sarah decided to just splash some water on her face, get dressed, and make up the bed. *I'll wait for Heather in the living room. Perhaps by then I'll come up with some kind of plan on how to proceed.*

CHAPTER TWENTY

Heather woke up to a quiet house. *Sarah must still be asleep. I'll try to not wake her until I've gotten ready.* Heather proceeded to get her shower, fix her hair and makeup and then dress for work. When she carefully opened the door to the master bedroom, there was no Sarah and the bed was made. In fact, it almost looked like it hadn't been slept in.

"Sarah? Are you up?"

"In here," came the reply.

Heather walked to the living room to find Sarah fully dressed, sitting on the couch with her purse next to her and looking very tired.

"Are you okay? You look pale. Are you sick?"

"No, no, just didn't get much sleep last night."

"Is something bothering you? Do you need to talk about it?"

"Heather, it's personal and I really do appreciate your offer but can I just keep it to myself? It's nothing that you can help me with. Trust me."

Heather looked concerned, "Well, okay, but if you need anything, promise me you'll ask. Okay?"

Sarah gave a weary smile, "Yes … I will. Thank you dear."

"All right, then, shall we take off?"

Sarah sighed and slowly rose off the couch, "Yes, no point in delaying."

Sarah remembered that Mike Ahmadi had said that he would call but with him on the other end of the phone line, well, it just felt like it would provide too easy an escape route if he refused to hear what she had to say. It would be better face to face. *Or worse*, she thought.

On the drive to town, Heather stole side glances at Sarah as she drove. Aside from the obvious fatigue, she looked concerned. *What did her visitor do or say to her? If someone tries to hurt this woman, I'll kill 'em!* As Sarah made the last turn to head into town she said,

"Heather, I forgot to ask you about last night. I thought I heard Mark's voice. Did you guys get to spend some fun time together?"

Heather couldn't suppress a smile, "Oh, yes, it was … delightful."

"That's nice," said Sarah off-handedly.

It didn't pass Heather's notice, "Are you sure you're okay?"

"Oh, my yes, yes dear. Please don't worry, I'll be all right. No need to fret."

"Okay, I just know that if I hadn't gotten any sleep, I'd be in way worse shape than you. You must have inherited good genes."

Of course, that's it! Sarah popped wide awake.

Heather wasn't sure she believed her but now Sarah seemed to buzz with energy. They had just arrived at the café but it was clear that Sarah was not open to any further discussion. Still, she couldn't help but be curious as to what could have transpired yesterday afternoon to make such a change in Sarah's demeaner. Heather hopped out of the car and walked into the café. But, instead of heading to the back to get her apron, she turned and stood next to the frame of the front window and peeked around the edge. She caught sight of Sarah backing out of the parking space and then, after changing gears, moving the car forward. She thought Sarah would be driving out of sight but instead went the short distance to the hotel and parked in front. *So, true to your note, you're meeting with your visitor.* Heather was brought up short by Mabel's voice,

"Heather! Table Six!"

* * *

When Mike Ahmadi woke up, it was early. His body still hadn't adjusted to Central Time, even though it was only one hour's difference. He took out his tablet and played Texas Hold 'Em for half an hour. In that time, he had won $25,000 and lost $30,000. It was virtual money but it reinforced his belief that gambling was for fools. He switched over to Spider Solitaire, single suit. It was an easy game but, despite not gambling with real money, he still liked to win.

When the clock displayed 8:00 am he took out his cell phone and tapped in the phone number that Ms. Bennington had given him yesterday before he left. It rang and rang but no one picked up.

"Well," he said to himself, "maybe she isn't awake yet. I'll watch a little TV and try later."

Tapping the power button to the remote, the TV came to life with the news from Amarillo. He had found the political news he watched in D.C. held his interest in a stomach-churning way but discussions of pork futures and wheat yields were the opposite end of the spectrum. *This is absolutely mind numbing.* He turned off the TV and went back to his tablet. The internet speed at the hotel was underwhelming but it was enough that he could read Google news without any problems. He realized that he had let time get away from him when he looked again at the clock and it was almost 9:30. He grabbed his phone and tapped redial. It still rang and rang with no answer. *That's odd. I'm sure that we agreed I would call her this morning.* No sooner had the thought cleared his mind than the hotel phone by the bed startled him with its loud bell.

He picked up the receiver and said, "Hello?"

"Yeah, Mr. Ahmadi, it's Donnie down at the desk. Sarah Bennington is here to see you. She says she'll wait in the hotel café for you."

Huh, this is unexpected but, "Okay, tell her I'll be down in 10 minutes."

"Yup, will do."

After hanging up, Mike puzzled out loud,

"Why wouldn't a phone call do?"

CHAPTER TWENTY-ONE

When Martin Acosta arrived at the Creek County Sheriff's Office, he followed his usual routine; turn on the computer, get coffee, scroll through emails. He was surprised to see one from Pete Wolfe. It was interesting and potentially exciting news given the subject line - *Heads Up*. The message read:

> **Martin,**
>
> **I stayed up late working on your 'head'. Once the CT scan was completed, the algorithms seemed to work quite well. I'm going to do a little more tweaking but should have an image for you sometime later this morning. Will shoot it along to this email address, so give me a confirmation reply back now. If you want me to use a different email address let me know. You should probably check your spam folder just in case. Til then.**
>
> **Pete**

Acosta smiled and rubbed his hands together, "Looks like we are making really fast progress here." He cocked his head and muttered, "But Pete, if your message went to my spam folder, how would I know to look there?" This was followed by a short snicker.

Well, anyway, here's hoping once I have it we can get an identification back from Antelope Valley. Acosta clicked on 'reply', typed 'thanks' and then hit 'send'.

He raised his coffee mug toward the monitor in a mock toast and took a sip of the hot sludge to seal the sentiment. Then a thought occurred to him. *I'd better give the guys over in Antelope Valley a 'heads up' on this too.*

Checking his watch, he figured there should be at least one person in the office at the Antelope Valley Police Station. He rechecked the number and then dialed. *I hope I don't have to put those guys on speed-dial.* After two rings, the voice on the other end confirmed he was right.

"Antelope Valley Police Station, Sergeant Mike Glatt."

"Hey, Mike, this is Martin Acosta."

"Oh, hey Martin, how are things going over there. Find any more body parts in … them there pahrts?"

"That was a horrible accent and no, we haven't. However, I do have some news for you guys."

"Oh, okay, what's up?"

"We're going to have a facial image on that head to send to you later this morning. At least according to the guy over at OSBI."

"No way. That's unbelievably fast. What, they have a sculptor sitting around waiting who doesn't need sleep?"

"I was surprised too. No, it's all done with computers. They didn't even need to deflesh the head. In fact, the guy, name's Pete, said he was actually looking for something like that for a grant study he was doing. Probably the reason why he jumped right on it."

"Wow … well, okay, appreciate you letting us know. I'll make sure to tell Mark about this when he gets in."

"Okay, Mike. Hope we can finally put an end

to this. Oh, by the way, tell Mark I still have a bruise on my ass thanks to him."

"HA! Will do, Martin, will do." Glatt was still chuckling after the call ended. Mark Stoner walked in a moment later.

Seeing Glatt, Mark asked, "What are you laughing about?"

Glatt smiled, "Well, two things. That was Martin Acosta on the phone just before you walked in. He said they're going to have an image for us later this morning."

Mark's eyebrows went up, "For that head they found?"

Glatt nodded.

"That was quick. Are they sure about what they did? I mean mistakes can be made, right? Especially if they hurry a job along. Are we sure it's the same head?" The meandering words came out in a rush. Mark was thinking ahead about Heather.

"Whoa, cowboy, what's with all the questions? The quick turnaround was my first ask. Apparently, they do this stuff with CT scans and computers." Seeing the look on Mark's face he added,

"Oh, you're worried about Heather aren't you?"

Mark frowned and nodded, "I'm not sure how she'll take it if it turns out to be Beaumont."

Glatt answered, "You're overthinking this. We know the arm and the head had a DNA match. I admit that's really strong evidence of it being him. BUT, we do not have confirmation. Sooo, let's take it one step at a time. The next step, as you well know, it getting Heather's verdict, whichever way. Besides, she's just as serious about you as you are about her."

Mark sighed, "I sure hope so." After a pause, he added, "What was the other thing?"

Glatt frowned, "What?"

"You said there were two things. So, what was the other thing?"

Glatt grinned, "He said to tell you he still has a bruise on his ass that you gave him playing football."

Mark absent-mindedly rubbed his chest. It was the place years ago where Martin Acosta drove his shoulder pad when he had tackled Mark. It was also the place where a pretty young lady had set up residence.

He responded, "I know the feeling ... you don't soon forget." He was thinking, though, *How will this affect Heather if it turns out it's HIM?*

CHAPTER TWENTY-TWO

After hanging up the phone at the front desk, Donnie walked over to the café section of the hotel lobby. He saw Sarah seated off to the left in a chair with its back to the wall and facing him as he approached. It almost looked like a defensive posture.

He stopped and rested his hands on the back of the chair facing her.

"Hey there, Sarah. Mr. Ahmadi says he'll be down in about ten."

As he turned to walk away, Sarah called after him, "Donnie? Excuse me, but would you have any Q-tip swabs and a few plastic Zip-Lock baggies I could use?"

Donnie paused and rubbed his chin, "Umm, ye-e-ah, yeah, I think I do actually. I'll check on the supplies at the front desk. I'll be right back."

"Thank you." Sarah hoped she could get the young man to go along. If he was willing to trust the science in spite of whatever emotional denials he might have, then the truth could come out. He would have to accept it. *I hope he'll accept it.*

Donnie returned with six Q-tips and four

sandwich sized baggies, "There ya go."

"Thanks, Donnie, that's perfect. Much appreciated."

"Sarah, if you're going to clean your ears or something, don't leave the wax or whatever else lying around. I hate lookin' at that shit." Donnie turned and began the short walk to the front desk.

Sarah nearly choked. Still within ear shot she said, "Oh, ah, okay, sure." *If there's a constant in this universe, it has got to be Donnie's mouth.*

Sarah was glad that she kept a Sharpie in her purse. She took it out and labeled four bags – two were marked *Sarah* and the other two *Mike*. Using two of the Q-tips, one at a time, she rubbed the head on the inside of her cheek for approximately thirty seconds and then placed it in the bag marked Sarah. The process was repeated again for the second bag. The notation "Sample taken" was added to each. She put the two extra swabs into her purse after first placing one each into the other bags, one of which she hoped, Mike would use for his own test. Now, all she needed was for him to agree to her plan.

Sarah raised up and peeked over the edge of

the planter bordering the café area and saw three persons in one body; Mike Ahmadi, Muhammad Nabul and Joseph Nabul all wrapped up in a son she hadn't seen except as a baby, a thirteen-year-old and now a full-grown man. Joy and ache swirled together like marbled cake. You couldn't focus on one without detecting the other. She saw Donnie point Mike Ahmadi toward where she was sitting.

She quickly sat and patted down the plastic bags on the small table. The bags didn't need her to do that but her nerves did. Then having them there made her nervous so she started to put them in her purse but then worried that she might somehow mix them up. *I'm like Buridan's Ass, a donkey stuck between two feed bags, frozen by indecision.* She left the plastic bags alone on the table. She hoped that this situation didn't end up in the same manner with the truth stuck somewhere between belief and proof. No sooner had that thought occurred than she was interrupted by Mike Ahmadi.

"Good Morning, Ms. Bennington."

CHAPTER TWENTY-THREE

At ten o'clock, Acosta called the Antelope Valley Police Station and got Mark Stoner this time.

"Antelope Valley Police Station, Officer Mark Stoner speaking."

"Hey, there Mark, Martin Acosta here."

"Hi, Martin. Mike said that you might be sending us something."

"Yep, that's why I'm calling. Getting ready to do that. Do you want to get it or should I send it to your regular email?"

Mark put his hand of the receiver's mouthpiece. "Mike … hey Mike. Martin wants to know where we want the image of that head reconstruction sent."

Glatt looked up and pointed at his desk monitor.

"Martin, send it to the email address you used earlier. Mike and I will be looking for it."

"Okay, Mark. Nice talking to you. You boys take care."

"Back at ya." With that, Stoner hung up the phone and stared at it for a few seconds. He struggled with wanting to see the image and wanting to never see it.

* * *

"Good morning, Mr. Ahmadi." Sarah smiled in spite of the nervousness and tenseness she felt.

"I've asked you to call me Mike," reproached Ahmadi with a gentle smile.

"Of course, Mike," replied Sarah, "Did you have a restful night?"

"Yes, thank you." *Of course not, you might know where an unknown half-brother of mine is and it's like pulling teeth to get the information out of you!*

"If I might inquire, Ms. Bennington. I did offer to call you, which I did in fact, but there was no answer. I was surprised when I was informed by Donnie that you were here. Is there some reason why we could not have talked by phone?"

"Well, yes, I think there is but before we get to that, I believe I owe you some further information from our last conversation."

Finally! "Very well, please go ahead."

Sarah recalled the brief history of Mike

Ahmadi's father and her going to college together. How they had gotten a small apartment and managed some classes along the way. She explained about their partnership in taking care of the newborn son, Joseph. At that point, the anxiousness in Ahmadi was palpable. Sarah explained that they had negotiated the name.

"Your father wanted to name him Muhammad, after himself. I wanted to name him Joseph after my grandfather. So, we compromised and named him Joseph Muhammad Nabul."

Makes sense, my father wanted a son name Muhammad so, after I was born, my naming must have been a foregone conclusion. "I see, but please tell me how my father ended up in Afghanistan and you and, I'm assuming Joseph, did not?"

He could see tears were starting to form in the woman's eyes.

"I'm sorry, I don't mean to be insensitive, but you can understand that this is quite important to me."

Sarah dried her eyes and looked down at the plastic bags with their Q-tips. Ahmadi followed her gaze and saw the bags lying in front of the woman.

Only now did he recognize the names on them and one of the names was his!

"Actually, Joseph was taken to Afghanistan by his father. I had no idea he had left with my son until I got home and found the note he had left." Now some tears had escaped and trailed down her cheeks. She pulled a tissue from her purse and dabbed at each eye.

Ahmadi slumped back in his chair, "My brother is dead. That's why my father never mentioned him to me."

Sarah drew a deep breath and let it out slowly, "No, Joseph Muhammad Nabul is very much alive, thank goodness."

Sarah could see that Ahmadi appeared perplexed. *His mind won't allow him to make the connection. I guess I have done all I can to gently lead him to it but now I just have to come out with it.*

Ahmadi blurted, "How can this be? It makes no sense! How do you know he's still alive?"

Sarah had to swallow the lump in her throat and after a brief pause said, "Because I'm looking at him."

Ahmadi response was stymied momentarily, "… Wait. What!? What are you saying?"

"You were born Joseph Muhammad Nabul. I-I …I'm your mother."

Ahmadi shook his head and swiveled sideways in his chair, "That cannot be. I've lived all of my first thirteen years in Afghanistan. What you say is impossible. Why are you doing this? What's in it for you in telling this lie?"

Sarah tried to stay calm, "I'm not lying and, I can prove it. If you're willing to accept my suggestion."

Ahmadi was mentally half out of his chair. Only his curiosity kept him seated. The woman seemed sincere but many mentally ill people can appear that way. *I guess it can't hurt to hear her out.*

With arms folded, he said, "I'm listening."

"I have two sets of bags here. One set with each of our names. I have taken swabs of my cheek and put one in each of the bags with my name. I am asking you to do the same for yours. I will send mine in for DNA comparison and, just so you don't have to trust me, you will be able to do the same."

Ahmadi stared at the woman for a few moments. It was preposterous but something in the back of his mind was nagging at him. Why did his father want him to find this stranger in a foreign country? It must have been more than just keeping him out of harm's way, otherwise he wouldn't have had to travel all this way. Could it have also been guilt at having separated a child from his mother? In spite of thinking it was a story for a pulp novel, he couldn't think of any harm since they would both have control of the same samples.

Ahmadi relented, "All right, what do I need to do?"

"Just rub the swab inside your cheek for thirty seconds or so and place it in the Zip-Lock bag with your name. Repeat it again for the second bag. We'll each take our set and then figure out how to share our information once we have the results back."

"Won't the samples go bad?"

"They shouldn't. From what I've heard, they'll be good for at least several months."

Ahmadi nodded, sighed, and proceeded to collect his samples. After zipping the second bag closed, he took his two bags and Sarah placed her two in her purse.

Ahmadi managed a weak smile, "Well, Ms. Bennington, I must admit that it's been … interesting. I need to go pack. It was nice meeting you."

Sarah scrambled to think of something to make the moment last longer.

"Oh, uh, since you've gone to so much trouble, let me treat you to lunch."

"It's really okay, you don't need to bother."

"Mr. Ahmadi, sorry, Mike, it's no bother at all. In fact, it's our custom here to always do this for visiting … friends from out of town."

"It will take me about a half hour."

"That's fine. I'll meet you just down the street at the Elkhorn Café. It's not the best place in town but it's about the ONLY place in town."

That quip made Ahmadi smile, he picked up his set of bags and said, "All right, thank you very much, Ms. Bennington." *My flight doesn't leave Will Rogers Airport until early evening. After a two-hour drive, I'll be waiting around for four hours or more. Might as well kill some of that time here as anywhere.*

Sarah watched her son walk away. *That went better than I thought. It must be difficult to find out that what you were convinced was true turns out NOT to have been.*

Sarah touched her set of bagged swabs before closing her purse. She rose from her chair and walked out to the lobby where she smiled and waved to Donnie. After exiting the hotel, she wondered how lunch would go. *What will we talk about? Will he be willing to talk?*

After returning to his room, Mike Ahmadi looked at the two bags in his hands.

"Eh, I'll wait 'til I'm on the road before I toss these. I don't want to risk upsetting the woman."

CHAPTER TWENTY-FOUR

Martin Acosta saw the new email in his inbox. It was from Pete Wolfe. It had the icon, which indicated an attached file. He didn't know why, but he took a deep breath before clicking it open. It read,

> *Officer Acosta,*
> *Please see the attached images. They show a left profile, full front and right profile image. My tweaking didn't do much at all, so am sending you the initial results. I hope this helps your case. Please make sure to let me know if you get a positive ID on this unfortunate person. My grant depends on it.*
> *Best Regards,*
> *Pete Wolfe*
> *P.S.: These are .jpg images. If you need higher resolution, I can provide them, just let me know.*

Martin saw that there were three files attached to the email. Each named with a case number hyphened with an ending number of one, two, and three respectively. Each carried the .jpg extension. He double-clicked on the first one. It was a left profile of a man's head. From what Martin could remember of the damaged head's hair color, it looked close, really close. He opened the next two in turn and found himself really impressed with the work Pete Wolfe had done. If this panned out, he was going to write a commendation letter for the guy.

"Well, Martin," he said to himself, "let's see if the boys in Antelope Valley can help us put this case to rest."

* * *

Sergeant Mike Glatt was halfway out of his chair when he noticed a new email arrive. Before he could settle back and read it, the phone rang.

"Antelope Valley Police Department, Sergeant Glatt speaking."

"Hey, Mike, it's Martin Acosta."

"Hey, Martin, I was just about to open the email you sent."

"Oh, good, you got it already. Well, I'm hoping you guys can help us out. I think it looks pretty good, but my opinion is worth about as much as tits on a boar. You'll get back to me as soon as you know something, yeah?"

"Ha, yep, sure thing. Mark is in back getting' a cup o' joe. I'll show it to him and then we'll make plans to get it in front of the person that might be able to make an identification."

"Okay, thanks a bunch. Talk to ya later."

"You got it. Bye," and with that salutation, Glatt hung up the phone. Mark walked in gently sipping his hot coffee.

Blowing across the mug, he asked Glatt, "Who was that?"

"Martin Acosta, he sent the image just now. Come on, you can view it with me."

Mark momentarily froze. Glatt pretended not to notice.

"Oh, there's three images here."

Mark walked over and stood behind Glatt's chair and waited while he opened the first file. What he saw was the left profile of a somewhat handsome man.

Glatt sat a little forward, "Well, seems whoever this is, he was a decent-looking guy."

Mark backhanded him on the shoulder.

"Come on, Mark. Whoever this is, is dead. I don't think you need to worry about him."

"I'm trying not to, Mike, it's just that the son-of-a-bitch seems to keep reaching beyond the grave."

'Well, we never did prove he was actually dead, not one hundred per-cent."

Mark had a miffed expression. He retorted, "You're not helping."

Glatt turned to face Mark, "We don't even know for *absolutely* certain that it's 'him', DNA match and all the other indicators notwithstanding. But, even if it turns out to be confirmed, isn't that a good thing? That means there's nothing left standing in the way of you gettin' your gal, right?"

Mark sighed, "Yeah, I guess." *Nothing in the way of me getting my gal except my gal.*

"All right, then, Mark, what say we go show these images to your Heather?"

Mark started to object but then realized it would just be putting off the inevitable. He sighed,

"Yeah … yeah, we might as well. Send a copy to my email and I'll show them to Heather with my phone."

"Okay, give me a sec."

"No rush. She's going to be working the noon meal today. Let's go over for an early lunch and do it. That way, it's not too busy, and she'll have something to occupy her mind if the picture ends up upsetting her."

"Eating your dad's cooking and caring about her feelings. You must have really fallen for this gal."

You don't know the half of it my friend. Mark looked at the wall clock. If they left now, they'd make it to the Elkhorn Café by 11:15. *Should be calm enough before the lunch crowd starts. But will it be calm for Heather?*

*   *   *

Sarah had sat in her car for more than twenty minutes, hoping to meet up with the man who, she knew in her heart, was her lost son returned to her by some miracle. The more she thought about it, the worse of an idea it seemed. She knew he had doubts. Clinging to him, as much as she ached to do so, would only serve to make him distance himself. Gathering her courage, she grabbed her purse and headed over to the Elkhorn.

Once she entered, she realized that she needed a restroom. Other than the brief dinner, when she first arrived in town, It had been so long ago, she was uncertain of the location of the ladies restroom. She thought it was on the left, just past the counter seating. Mabel looked up and saw Sarah mouth the word, *Bath-room.* Mabel smiled and pointed to the left side of the counter. *It was where I thought it was!* It seemed silly to Sarah to consider this a victory, but she was grasping at anything that might indicate things would be going her way. After entering the bathroom, locking the door and sitting down, she tried to think of anything else that could convince her son to get the swabs tested for matching DNA. After several minutes, all that was left in her mind was a glum thought, *I can't think of a single thing.*

* * *

Mike Ahmadi paid his bill, thanked Donnie, and rolled his suitcase, with the carryon riding shotgun, out to his car. After opening the trunk and loading his luggage, he offloaded the messenger bag from his shoulder and placed it in the front passenger seat. He closed the door and shut the trunk lid. He patted his pockets out of habit. Car keys, check. Wallet, check. After locking the car, he looked up at the sky, a beautiful blue interrupted by cotton ball clouds that belied the heat and humidity he could already feel. He let out a sigh and began the short walk to the Elkhorn Café.

When Ahmadi entered the café, there were only a couple of patrons and those few appeared to be chatting and nursing cups of coffee. He checked his watch. *Well, it's only a little after eleven.* He looked around, but it was clear that Sarah Bennington was not here yet.

"Sit anywhere you want, hon," said Mabel.

Ahmadi smiled, *That must be what they call southern hospitality*, "Thank you."

He decided to take a position in the middle of the counter seating. The swiveling stools would allow him mobility to see and put him in the center so Sarah would have no trouble spotting him.

Heather approached the stranger who had just arrived at the counter.

"Ready to order or do you need a minute?"

"Oh, I'm waiting for someone." Checking his watch, Ahmadi continued, "I'm early so it may be a bit."

"Not a problem. Can I start you off with something to drink while you're waiting?"

"Sure, can I have some hot tea?"

"Comin' right up."

After placing the miniature tea kettle of hot water, tea bag and cup in front of Ahmadi, Heather said,

"There you go. If you need anything else, just let me know."

"Thanks, will do," replied Ahmadi as he watched the young lady leave and go back into the kitchen area.

* * *

Mark Stoner and Mike Glatt walked into the Elkhorn Café. Mark held the door open for two couples to enter and then looked around the eatery. Other than those townspeople, Mark saw several residents who had already established squatter's rights at their table and some guy he didn't know sitting at the counter. There was no Heather.

"She must be in back."

Glatt asked, "Why don't you go get her?"

"I don't want to intrude," lied Stoner.

Glatt wasn't fooled, "Well, let's take this table by the front window. We're in no rush. After all, we've got your dad's cooking to look forward to."

As they sat down, Glatt could see that his humor didn't relax Mark. *Poor guy is on pins and needles. I hope she turns out to be as nice as she appears. She could twist Mark around her little finger. In fact, I bet HE would do the twisting!*

Just then, Heather walked back from the kitchen, and spotting Mark, broke into a big grin. Mark got up and started walking toward her. As he approached, she could see his face more clearly, and it made her smile begin to fade.

"Mark, what is it? Are you okay?"

He nodded, "I have something to tell you. And … I also have something I need you to look at."

"Oh, um, okay, I guess."

"Let's go back to the kitchen."

As they walked into the kitchen area, Mark guided Heather to the small office space to the right where the books and other business matters of the café were conducted. Mark sat in the office chair and Heather sat in the side chair beside the desk.

"What is it, Mark?"

"I know you've been down a long road with … everything. Well, it turns out that, over in an eastern county, they found some remains."

Heather started to squirm, "o-okay."

"The thing is, DNA testing was done and it matched the DNA from the arm that we found in the field near the Bennington place."

Heather's hand went to her mouth.

"Now, I'm not asking you to look at anything bad, like before. And, given the circumstances, unlikely as it may seem, if it were your husband, we believe that you are the only person who can confirm it."

"I don't understand, how will a body part be identifiable by me?"

"It's a man's head."

Heather immediately started turning pale.

Mark leaned forward quickly and put his hand on her arm, "We're not asking you to look at the remains. A facial reconstruction was done and I have the images on my phone. We're hoping you can give us a yes or no regarding identification. Would you do that for us?"

"No … but for you, yes."

"Okay, give me just a sec' and I'll pull up the images."

Heather could feel butterflies and knots wrestling around in her stomach. *If it turns out to be him, how will I deal with … that?*

Mark started turning the phone toward Heather, "Okay, here's the front view of the face but I have both profiles as well if you need it."

Heather instantly recognized the face of the man who had abused her and made her life a living hell. It still sent a shock through her. She tried to control herself but a tear escaped her left eye as she nodded.

When she finally found her voice she said, "Yes … yes, that's him. His hair was never kept that neat but it's definitely him. That's the face of Roger Beaumont."

Mark asked sympathetically, "You're sure? I

need to make certain."

Heather grabbed a tissue from the desk and dabbed at her eye, "Yes, Yes, I'm certain, beyond any doubt."

"All right. In a day or so, we'll need you to sign a statement. I'll keep in touch about that." Mark kept his eyes on Heather as he put away his phone, "Are you okay?"

Heather nodded, "Yes, I just need a moment. Please, just a moment … to myself,"

Mark replied, "All right. I'll be out front."

After Mark left, Mabel came over. She could see that Heather was bothered by something.

"Heather, hon, are you okay? Do you need to go home sick?"

"No, no, I just got some news."

That raised Mabel's eyebrows, "Good news, I hope."

"Well, yes, a problem I thought I might still have, I no longer have. The odd thing is, it's like a piece of my life is now missing, the piece that the problem occupied. Kind of like a piece to a jigsaw puzzle that used to be in the box but no longer can be found."

"Sudden changes take time to get used to," said Mabel somberly. Then brightening, she added, "When I have a missing puzzle piece, I make a piece to fit in that space. It's not the same as the original but at least I no longer have a hole in my puzzle."

Heather looked wide-eyed at Mabel, "Mabel, you are a wise woman."

Mable thought, *I would make an even wiser Mother-in-Law*, but instead said, "Listen, why don't you go ahead and take your break now. We won't be in a rush for at least a half-hour."

Heather nodded, "Thank you, Mabel, I'll do that."

*   *   *

As Mark began walking back to the table. Mike Glatt couldn't tell whether the photo had upset Heather or not. Before Mark got near to him, Mike spotted movement out of the corner of his eye. He turned to look out the café window. A man partially obscured by the tempera paint declaring the café's specials, made his identity uncertain. One thing was sure, though, the guy was wearing a long coat in hot weather. He could also tell by the guy's eyes that something or someone in the restaurant was making him upset. When the man turned to walk away, he could see that it was Joss Poltroon.

When Mark sat down, Mike's attention turned, "So, what's the verdict?"

"She confirmed it's definitely Roger Beaumont."

"No kidding? Man, that's gonna make Acosta happy."

Mark nodded, "Yep, I even asked her to confirm and she did."

"Was she upset?"

"I'm not sure. She asked for some time to be by herself."

"Hmm, not good, but then not bad…Oh, hey, guess who I saw standing outside?

Mark leaned back in his chair as he waited for some lame comment, "Okay, I give. Who?"

"Joss Poltroon. Wasn't he a classmate of yours in high school?"

"He was an *ass-hole* classmate of mine in high school, so?"

"Really, how come you say that?"

"Well, that was back in the day when Dad was teaching, before he decided to retire and take over the café here. Joss knew that since my Dad was a teacher, you know how dependent teachers are in a small community like this and the politics involved, Joss could harass me any time he wanted and there was nothing I could do about it. Not, that is, without causing some serious trouble. He was always on my case. 'Better watch yourself, Stoney. I'm a gonna haf'ta' slap you up the side a' the head, Stoney.' Bull crap like that. If I was carrying around a basketball, he'd knock it out of my hands. He was just a turd. When we had football practice, he'd wait until two other guys slowed me down and THEN he'd run in to join the tackle. It was like getting bumped by a gnat."

"Does he suffer from any medical condition?"

"Hell, if I know. Why are you asking me this stuff?"

"When I saw him just a minute ago. It looked like he was casing the place."

Mark snorted, "Well, if he thinks this is the town bank, he's going to very disappointed."

"He didn't seem very happy. In fact, I'd swear he was angry about something."

Mark looked at Glatt like he was listening to crazy George Pearson, "Who gives a flyin' flip?"

"Also, he was wearing a long coat."

"In *this* weather?"

"Yeah, curious, isn't it?"

"Yeah, but I'm not going to waste any more brain time on that jerk. He doesn't deserve it."

"Well, if it's all the same to you, I'm going to keep an eye out for the guy. Something doesn't feel right."

* * *

Josser "Joss" Leroy Poltroon was a failure. He hadn't always been. His father was a very successful farmer and rancher known throughout the county for his Black Angus cattle. Joss, it seemed, won Grand Champion every year at the State Fair. Banks and Insurance Agencies would bid on show cattle to use for advertising. Joss got to collect a tidy sum. His junior year of high school, he bought a sweet, black Chevrolet Bel Air Super-Sport. His senior year he traded it in and got a Pontiac GTO with big block V-8 engine. When he punched it, your head would get flung back from the sudden acceleration. Mark had managed, combining his money with a little added from his dad, to get an eight-year-old Dodge four-door sedan. He had begrudgingly admitted to himself that he was jealous of Joss.

But Joss's days, it turned out, were numbered. After his father passed away, his mother expected him to manage the farm and the cattle. Unfortunately for Joss, he had concentrated on being the big man at high school and trying to impress his girlfriend, and everyone else, with his hot car. His lack of experience and understanding of modern agriculture resulted in the farm falling into ruin. It was only a few months after selling the mineral rights to help make ends meet, that natural gas was discovered in the area. Someone else would be getting the royalties. He felt he'd been robbed. Life was so fucking unfair!

Joss had seen the man enter the Elkhorn and couldn't believe his eyes. *Was that a fucking beaner that just walked in?* He made a pass by the window just a little after the two city policemen entered. He had been so self-involved after high school; he didn't recognize a former classmate.

He muttered to himself, "I'll be damned. No one has any common sense anymore. They'll let these wetback beaners go anywhere. They need to be sent back to their own country and stop fucking up ours."

He made a decision. He turned and walked back to his pickup. Opening the toolbox storage unit in the truck bed, he took out his long coat that he used for bad weather. After putting it on, he opened the driver side door and pitched the seatback forward to retrieve the thirty-aught-six rifle that he kept there. He picked up the box of bullets that nestled nearby. After loading four bullets into the weapon, he put it under the coat, holding it with his right hand now slipped through the faux pocket. From what he could see, it was well hidden. He returned to the café.

Standing in front once again, he peered through a clear spot past all the dumb-ass paint and found his target sitting at the counter. Right in the goddam middle! He walked back to his pickup, uncertain whether to go through with it. But then, he thought to himself, *You fuckin' wetback. You come here to rape our women, commit murder, deal drugs and steal our jobs. It's just like I heard over and over on TV. And now, here you are, plantin' your brown ass down in my home town, as if you own the place. Well, today is one UN-fuckin' lucky day for you. Someone has ta' take care of pests like you an' I'm just the 'merican can do it!*

Poltroon reasserted his grip on the weapon, walked back muttering to himself, opened the door, and entered the Elkhorn Café'.

CHAPTER TWENTY-FIVE

Mike Glatt was facing the entry to the café and Mark was facing Mike. Glatt spotted Joss as he entered. He leaned toward Mark and said, "You're not gonna' believe who just walked in." Mark glanced over his left shoulder to see Joss Poltroon, in his long coat, staring forward. He turned back to Mike and gave a, "Hmph."

It was a only a split second later that Glatt saw the end of a rifle barrel peeking out from the bottom of Joss Poltroon's coat. His reaction was immediate, "GUN!"

Glatt tried to bolt from his chair but the rotund Mrs. McClary had taken a seat right behind him and was slow to move. He was stymied. Mark spun around as he exited his chair and saw his high school nemesis start to raise a rifle, apparently intending to aim it toward the front of the restaurant. The direction, it appeared to him, where his sweetheart was now entering. He bolted like a man shot out of a cannon. All the intimidation, bullying and abuse he had suffered at the hands of this bastard flashed front and center in his mind and now he was trying to kill

the woman he loved!? Mark was instantly trans-
formed into a raging bull.

* * *

Sarah had given up trying to comprise
anything to engage the young man, her son, in
meaningful dialogue. Even now, that word caused a
catch in her breathing. Sighing, she gave the toilet a
flush, washed her hands and checked her face in the
mirror. She looked every bit as tired as Heather had
implied earlier. *Well, I can't put this off any longer.*
She exited the Ladies Restroom.

* * *

Mike Ahmadi noticed the movement to his
left and saw Sarah Bennington come through the door
from the Ladies Restroom. He swiveled slightly and
the movement caused the napkin on his left leg to fall.
He bent over to retrieve it.

* * *

Heather had come back from her break and
saw Sarah rushing with arms outstretched. She turned
quickly to her left to see what Sarah was reacting to
and saw a man with a rifle aiming at Sarah!

Heather ran, arms out, toward Sarah

screaming, "Nooooooo!" Sarah ran to shield Mike
Ahmadi screaming, "Nooooooo!"

* * *

Mark Stoner hit Poltroon at full speed, lifting
the man off his feet and smashing him into the wall
next to the jukebox. Poltroon had managed to cock
the lever action Springfield and it discharged as he
attempted to swing it around to the right, in a
defensive reflex, toward the charging policeman. The
bullet went above the heads of the two women and
man at the counter. It ricocheted off the stainless-steel
order slip carousel sending it spinning and orders
slips flying. It ended its trajectory by lodging in the
ceiling air conditioning vent.

The gun dropped to the floor. The unconscious Joss Poltroon did as well. Mark was in an
unbridled rage. *The bastard could have killed
Heather!* He had pulled his service weapon as soon as
Joss had hit the floor. He was pressing the barrel into
the man's temple. The skin on Poltroon's head started
to ooze blood around the edges of the barrel. *Oh, how
I want to end you!* It was then that a voice managed to
intrude.

"Mark! Mark, it's okay. He's not going anywhere. Put away your weapon. I've got him. I'll cuff him and load him in the cruiser. Go take care of Heather."

Mark realized that he was breathing heavily and his heart was pounding. He jumped up, holstered his weapon and jogged passed the handful of patrons, who were now frozen where they sat, to where Sarah Bennington, Heather and a man he didn't recognize were all crouched down on the floor by the counter stools.

Mark asked urgently, "Heather are you okay?" He then turned to the other two, "Are you guys all right?"

Heather said, "Thanks to you we are." She then leaned over and gave Mark a quick hug.

Mark went table to table and checked on the other customers, "Are you folks okay? Are you doing all right? Everything good here?" They all responded with slow nods. Walking back to the threesome who were the apparent targets of Poltroon, he asked, "Ms. Bennington are you all right?"

Sarah turned to Ahmadi and said, "Yes, I

seem to be fine. Jos … um, Mike, are you okay?"

Ahmadi replied, "Yes, except my nerves are frayed. What the hell was *that* about?"

Mark said, "We won't know for sure until we interrogate him but it appeared he was after one of you. Heather, any chance you know Joss Poltroon?" Heather shook her head.

"Ms. Bennington?"

"Sorry, Mark, the people I know, with very few exceptions are from my school days." She saw Mark looking at Mike Ahmadi. "Oh, Mark, Heather, this is my … friend, Mike Ahmadi. He's visiting from out of town."

"Pleased to make your acquaintance, Mr. Ahmadi," said Mark. *I wonder what the connection is between Joss and this guy. Seems like he might have been the target … for some reason.*

"Please, call me Mike."

"Sure thing, Mike. I hope you won't let this unfortunate circumstance interfere with your time visiting. This kind of thing … just doesn't happen around here."

"Actually, I was getting ready to head back

home. Just stopped to have lunch with my … friend," indicating Sarah, "before I take off."

Mark nodded, "Well, it seems you guys are unharmed … at least physically. I'm going to go in back and see if my parents have recuperated from having been scared to death."

As he rose to stand, Mark asked, "Mr. Ahmadi, I probably won't need it, but since you're leaving, would you give me your cell phone number? Just in case."

Ahmadi replied while pulling out his wallet, "Sure, here's my business card. That's my cell that I carry all the time. The email I check at least daily."

Once that transaction was completed, Mike Ahmadi watched the officer head toward the kitchen area. He turned back to face Sarah and Heather.

"Why did you two rush out like that? You could have been shot."

"I just felt the need to protect you."

Heather nodded, "And I just felt the need to protect Sarah."

Sarah Bennington smiled and squeezed Heather's hand. "I guess our Maternal instincts kicked in."

Ahmadi remained silent. *This woman potentially threw herself in front of a bullet to protect me. Either she's delusional about me or ...?*

They all three rose off the floor. Mike Ahmadi said, "Well, I'd better get going."

Sarah asked, "Can't you stay a little longer? We were supposed to have lunch."

"I think we both need some quiet time after ... *this*. I can get something on the road."

Heather had an idea, "I can get you a to-go order. How about that? Won't take long."

Ahmadi sighed, "Okay. How long would that be?"

Heather replied, "If you're okay with a sandwich and chips, we can have it ready for you in ten minutes."

Ahmadi paused and then relented, "All right, add an iced tea to go and ... I suppose that'll be all right."

Heather winked at Sarah.

Mark came back out and walked over to Sarah and Heather. Ahmadi had taken a seat at the counter.

"Okay, mom and dad are swearing off coffee for the rest of the day, maybe the week. I think their nerves will be back to abnormal by tomorrow."

Heather smiled and then turning to Mike said, "Mr. Ahmadi, I'll get that order in for you right now."

Mark said, "Heather, I've got to get going. There'll be a ton of paperwork. I'll be in contact with you later about … that other thing."

Heather walked over and planted a kiss on Mark, "I'll look forward to seeing you again, officer."

With that, Heather walked back to the kitchen. Mark was smiling and he noticed that Sarah was smiling as well. He couldn't suppress the mild blush he felt creeping up his neck. He nodded toward Sarah, bid Mike Ahmadi a good day and left to join Glatt in the police cruiser along with the asshole that had nearly ruined their lives.

* * *

Sarah took the few minutes that the 'to-go order' was taking to chat with her son, Mike Ahmadi, the former Muhammad Nabul and former Joseph Nabul. Talking about his work seemed like the best strategy. He seemed willing to talk about it. Sarah had to admit she didn't really understand much of it, most of it, well, all of it, but it was nice just to hear his voice and see the handsome man he had grown up to be. *Against all odds*, she thought, *against all odds*.

Heather walked out of the kitchen with a brown paper bag holding the sandwich order with chips and a sixteen-ounce Styrofoam drink container with lid, full of iced tea.

As she handed it to him, she said, "That will be $12.98. Straw is in the bag."

"Thank you."

Sarah interjected, "Heather, I promised him lunch so you can give me the ticket."

Ahmadi objected, "Ms. Bennington, you do not need to do that … really."

Sarah held up her hand, "It's our custom, remember? Besides, I insist." With that comment she handed Heather a twenty-dollar bill, "Keep the change." Before Heather could say anything, she added with a wink, "And no comment from you."

Heather started to walk away but Sarah touched her arm, "How are the folks in back?" She nodded toward the kitchen.

Heather paused a second, "Well, they were pretty shook-up. Nothing of importance was damaged. It was early, so there were only a few order slips and they were easily reorganized. The only difference was that everyone decided to have extra cheese added to their hamburgers and change their side order to large fries. Apparently, everyone decided to use the 'eat until my nerves are calm' method."

Sarah nodded, "I get that, but I'm surprised they didn't close down for the day."

Heather stepped closer and spoke in a low tone, "I don't think they can really afford to. Mabel had shared that restaurants operate on a slim margin. With the addition of fast-food places around town, it's gotten even harder."

Sarah nodded, "Okay, well, I'm going to go home and feed the chickens. I'll drive back and pick you up from work, okay?"

As Heather started walking back toward the kitchen, she said, "Sounds good, Sarah. See you then."

Sarah saw that Mike Ahmadi was anxious

to hit the road, "So, are you off for your return trip?"

Mike Ahmadi nodded, "Yes, yes I am. It's been … interesting. I wish you well, Ms. Bennington. Take care." He started to leave.

Sarah said, "Oh, let me walk you to your car."

This woman will just NOT let go. "All right, as you wish."

No words were shared as they walked the short distance. Ahmadi opened the car door and, after sliding in, placed his lunch bag in the adjoining seat next to his messenger bag and the drink into the middle console cup holder.

"Well, I'm off. Thank you for lunch and the … excitement."

"It was my pleasure … the lunch, not the other. Oh, before I forget, would you give me one of your business cards? I'd like to stay in touch regarding the DNA results."

Oh dear. "Okay, yes." He retrieved his wallet and pulled out a card. "Of course, that's my business address but the cell number, as I mentioned to the police officer, is for the phone I'm carrying. In case you need to call." *Why on earth did I just suggest that?*

Sarah looked at the card. At least she had this to look at even if it turned out she would not see her son again. *I dearly hope that's not the case.* "Thank you, Mike. I won't forget you."

Ahmadi nodded, started the car and backed out, beginning his trip back home. He watched the woman shrink in his rear-view mirror.

Somehow, he thought, *I have a feeling I won't be forgetting you either.*

CHAPTER TWENTY-SIX

After returning to the farm, Sarah spent the afternoon pondering what a crazy day it had turned out to be, but mostly she thought about her son. She hoped he would follow through, but even if he didn't, she had her set of swabs. One way or the other she would put the information in front of him. The problem was that she had no control over what would happen afterward. She fretted even though there was nothing to fret about yet and the obvious truth that doing so would accomplish exactly nothing.

She had fed the chickens. *Egg collecting can wait until tomorrow morning. Might as well drive into town and pick up Heather, it's late enough.*

During the drive, she felt fatigued, *I just don't have the energy to cook tonight. I'm going to have dinner at the Elkhorn. Maybe Heather will be willing to join me.*

Upon approaching the café, she saw a half dozen people standing around the entrance. *What in the world is going on there?*

Sarah had to park her car half a block away as there were no available spaces in front. She walked to the café and realized that she recognized no one there. She addressed a gray-haired gentleman and his wife who were nearest to her.

"Excuse me, but is there a problem?"

"I'll say," growled the man. "There's a 45-minute wait!"

"What?" replied Sarah.

The man nodded and said, "Yeah, I can't believe it either, but everyone wants to see where the shootout occurred." Apparently, the discharge of a rifle had gained somewhat in reputation.

Sarah looked through the front window and saw that every table was occupied with at least two people. A couple of the tables had six customers trying to make four positions work. She finally spotted Heather running from table to table. A lock of hair had fallen down across her eye and she had to keep pushing it with the hand holding her pen or else blow out the side of her mouth while writing. She looked up and spotted Sarah.

Heather mouthed, "Sor-ry" and gave a short gesture of "see what's around me?"

Sarah mouthed, "Ho-tel" and pointed in that

direction. Heather gave her a thumbs up.

As Sarah walked toward the hotel, she wondered what story Heather would have for her when she managed to show up. As usual, after she entered, she spotted Donnie at the front desk.

He spotted her and smiled, "Hey there, Sarah, back for more swabs & bags?"

Sarah chuckled slightly, "No, not for that. The café is really busy and there's a long wait. Can I get a bite to eat? Please?"

Donnie's smile slipped, "I heard about all the commotion that went on over there. Some kind of gunplay. Well, you know we're more like a B&B."

Shootout? Gunplay? Sarah nodded, "Yes, but I'm hungry and boy, do I NOT feel like cooking."

Donnie nodded, "I hear ya. Well, what are you hungry for?"

"Can I get a hamburger?"

"Nope."

"Oh, well, a burrito?"

"Nope."

"All right, let's cut to the chase. What can you fix for me?"

"I don't get my breakfast supplies until early tomorrow morning. So, I've got whole wheat bread, bologna, Miracle Whip, American cheese slices and for an accompanying vegetable, pork and beans."

"Any chance you could fry the bologna?"

"Y-e-a-h, yeah I can do that."

"Okay, it's a deal." As Donnie started to walk away, Sarah added, "Do you have lettuce you can add to the sandwich?"

Donnie snorted, "As if."

Sarah walked over and sat down in the seat she had occupied earlier. *Okay, so no-o-o lettuce.*

It only took 15 minutes for Donnie to return with the sandwich and sloppy portion of pork and beans. As he sat the plate down in front of Sarah, he said,

"I forgot to ask. Did you want something to drink with your meal?"

He calls this a meal? "Yes, I'd like a beer."

"What kind would you like?"

Oh boy, not this again. "What kind do you have?"

His answer surprised her, "Let's see, there's

Bud Light, Budweiser, Skol, Yanjing, Heineken, Harbin, Brahma, Coors Light, Tsingtao and Snow."

"Wait a minute, you have all those brands of beer but all you can scrape together for food is a fried bologna sandwich?"

"Sarah, folks don't come here for dinner with the Elkhorn right down the street. They do want to drink, however. So, I get my margin where I can. So, what's it to be?"

"Coors Light, please."

"You got it."

Donnie walked back past a two-stool counter and through the adjacent passageway that served as the entrance to the kitchen area.

Sarah took a look at the sandwich. It was really substantial. Three slices of fried bologna with two slices of cheese melted between two slices of toasted wheat bread slathered with Miracle Whip. She took a bite and was instantly transported into the past. Her grandma had made her a similar sandwich in her tiny kitchen the day after her parents' funeral. The memories were swirling and tears were starting to cascade.

"Oh my god! What a day!" Heather had arrived unseen by Sarah and plopped down in a chair next to her. Heather looked like someone had chased her across the county and hosed her down afterwards. The abrupt arrival knocked Sarah from her reminiscing. Then, Heather noticed the tears.

"Sarah, are you okay?"

"Just a hot sandwich. Made my eyes water."

Donnie arrived with Sarah's beer. After setting it down he said, "Heather, right?"

Heather smiled, "Yep, that's right."

"Would you like something?"

Heather pointed at Sarah's glistening bottle, "That looks good. Bring me one of those?"

After Donnie left, Heather looked at Sarah and said, "I may need a couple of beers before we go."

Sarah sat up straighter, "Heather, I was going to have dinner at the Elkhorn but I couldn't believe how many people were there."

"I KNOW! It was crazy. Ed and Mabel briefly discussed shutting down for the day, you know, given all that happened but the word of the shooting got around like greased lightning. Folks started pouring in. They kept asking if this was the place where the shooting took place. It was unbelievable. I'm happy for the all the business it brought them but I sure hope tomorrow is slower."

Donnie arrived with Heather's beverage and, after she gave him a quick thanks, proceeded to gulp down half of the bottle's contents before she stopped to breathe. When she did, she looked at Donnie and said,

"Yep, I'm gonna need another one of these."

Donnie nodded and walked back to the kitchen area.

Heather looked at Sarah and noticed the odd sandwich she was eating. *And with pork and beans?*

"That looks like an interesting sandwich. It *is* a sandwich, right?"

Sarah smiled, "Yes, it's like the ones my grandmother would make for me from time to time. Fried bologna."

"Ugh. Really?"

"Well, it's better than it looks. Donnie's hotel is more like a B&B and he doesn't get breakfast supplies until tomorrow morning. I was really hungry and this is what he came up with."

Heather nodded and then posed the question she had been itching to ask,

"So, if you don't mind my being a nosy snoop, how did you come to know Mr. Ahmadi?"

Sarah sat silent for a moment. *This is a small community. When I get the DNA test done, what are the chances that I can keep everything quiet? Do I really want to keep it quiet, the fact that I have a son? Shouldn't I be proud and grateful? Do I really care if folks in town wouldn't approve? What business is it of theirs, anyway?*

"Sarah, I'm sorry … if it's a touchy subject. You can forget I asked. I didn't mean to upset you."

"No, Heather, it's okay. It's just … well, I … I knew him when he was a baby. But I didn't see him again until he was about 13 years old. And, now, after all these years I got to see him these past couple of days."

Heather looked puzzled, "Wow, he looked to be in his mid-thirties. You must mean a lot for him to travel all this way after what … twenty years?"

Something leaked inside Sarah's mind.

Looking down, she blurted, "He's my son."

Heather's jaw nearly hit the table. Neither of them had noticed Donnie's arrival with Heather's second beer, which he almost dropped. His approach was quiet but his response wasn't.

"ARE YOU SHITTING ME!?"

CHAPTER TWENTY-SEVEN

Mike Glatt and Mark Stoner had been on their way to the Medical Center when their 'passenger' in the back had roused from being unconscious.

Joss let out a small moan, "Got a headache. You pigs got any aspirin?"

Mike thought it would be a good idea to have Mark drive. He thought it might help calm him down a bit after the altercation at his parents' café. Mike indicated to Mark that they might be going to the police station holding cell instead and motioned for him to slow down. Mike turned slightly in his seat so he could see Joss Poltroon.

"Hey, Joss. Can you understand me? Can you hear me okay?"

"Yeeaah," came the slow response, "Why you askin'?"

"Since you're in our custody, I need to read you your Miranda Rights. You understand?"

"Yeah, don't know why, though. I should be gettin' a medal. Tryin' to protect my country."

Mark shook his head slightly. *What the hell is wrong with this jackass?*

Glatt proceeded, "Okay. You have the right to remain silent. You do not have to answer any questions or make any statements. Anything you say can be used against you in court. You have the right to a lawyer before we ask you any questions and you have the right to have him with you during the questioning. If you want to answer questions now, without a lawyer present, you may do so. You have the right to stop questions at any time."

Glatt paused to give Poltroon a moment to consider what was being said, "Do you understand the rights I have just spoken to you?"

Poltroon looked at Glatt and said, "Yeah."

"Is there anything you want to say at this time?"

Poltroon nearly spat the word, "LAW-YER!"

Not another word was spoken in the police cruiser the rest of the way to the police station. Glatt called for an EMT visit. They could examine him for a concussion rather than having the extra expense of taking the guy through the E.D. and so forth.

After getting Poltroon checked out and placing him in the holding cell, Glatt walked back to his desk and sat down. He noticed Mark was at his desk making a phone call.

"Calling to check up on Heather?"

"Naw, calling up my Uncle Frank. See if he's willing to take on a pro-bono case."

"You're asking your uncle to help out that ass-hat?"

"Yep."

Glatt look surprised. He shook his head and said, "THIS you need to explain."

Mark held up his index finger, "Uncle Frank? Yeah, it's me. No, stop calling me that. There is no "ie" at the end of my name … thank you. Listen, the reason for my call is, I'm wondering if you can take on a pro-bono case. It's Joss Poltroon … yeah, *that* guy."

Mark put his hand over the handset, "He's already heard about it. Guess word really gets around." Removing his hand, Mark continued," Yeah, we're holding him down here at the station. Yes, yes, he's asked for a lawyer. Okay, sounds good. We'll let Joss know you'll be coming by tomorrow morning. Oh, and thanks, Uncle Frank. Appreciate it."

Glatt's face looked like he had sat on a cattle prod, "Thanks? Appreciate it?"

After hanging up the phone, Mark walked around his desk and sat on the corner,

"Look. A public defender improbably but possibly could get the case screwed up if someone claims incompetent counsel. This way, he gets a good lawyer. I'm going to strongly suggest to the DA that they file charges of Attempted Murder, discharging a weapon within city limits and anything else we can come up with. Uncle Paul will negotiate down to felony assault with a deadly weapon and Joss Poltroon," Mark started counting with his fingers, "One, will be a convicted felon. Two, go to jail for sure. Three, he'll go to jail knowing that he owes me for getting my uncle to be his attorney free of charge. A trifecta."

Glatt slowly nodded, "Remind me to never piss you off."

* * *

After having sworn Donnie to secrecy, and that bit of irony was not lost on Sarah, she told Heather that she would drive. Sarah could see that

Heather's fatigue, coupled with the third beer she had finished minutes ago on an empty stomach, had 'relaxed' her. *Besides*, thought Sarah, *Heather certainly could use some rest after today*. They wasn't much discussion on the drive home.

Before getting out of the car, Sarah reached into her purse and took out the bagged cotton swabs. As she looked at them, she was pretty sure that a 23&ME test was not what was needed but also not sure how to proceed. Heather was groggy but not so much as not to notice Sarah. Heather noticed there was some kind of writing on the bags.

"Q-tips in a baggie? Whassup with that?"

"I think we need to get you to bed."

"'K, but what's …"

"I need to get a DNA test done. Well, actually two."

"Oh." Then Heather frowned, "But, you said he-uz your son. Why wouldja need a DNA test?"

"Well, it's a very long story. Let's just say that there's a request for confirmation."

"I see. Like checkin' two differ'nt things an' seein' if they're the same."

"Well, um, yes, a little like that, I suppose."

"I bet Mark can help ya with that."

Sarah looked surprised and then her eyes went wide, "Of course, he helped you with … your issue."

Heather winked and pointed her finger like it was the barrel of a handgun.

"I'll talk to him in the morning. Let's get both of us to bed. I'm exhausted." Sarah watched Heather as she walked somewhat steadily toward the farmhouse. She was going to make it, but not quickly.

CHAPTER TWENTY-EIGHT

Mike Ahmadi had indeed arrived at Will Rogers airport early. After checking luggage and clearing TSA security, finding a seat at one of the fast-food services was the next order of business. He ordered an iced tea. He wasn't all that thirsty, but having something in hand to twiddle with helped relieve tension. He was pondering what to do. The baggies with the swabs had been placed in his carry-on bag.

I have no real reason to follow through with her request. My father asked me to find her and I did. My obligation has been met. But the question of *why* still nagged at him. *What can getting the DNA results matter? You can always throw them away. You don't even have to contact her again.* It was like having two different angels on his shoulders debating back and forth. *But what will you do if the results show you come from the same blood? On the other hand, if it does match, wouldn't you want to know that?*

"Shut up!" Ahmadi realized that he had said this out loud. The other patrons gave him funny looks. He thought maybe it was time to move over to the departing gate. He looked at the number stamped on his ticket, dumped his tea and adjusting his carryon's strap, proceeded the short distance to his gate.

As he sat down he thought about his brother. It had been a while since he had last spoken to Karam. He seemed to recall that Karam had mentioned a friend who worked in a genetic testing lab. *Maybe Karam can help me out.* As he thought through this, he failed to consciously acknowledge that he had reached a decision. *Yes, tomorrow, I will give Karam a call.*

* * *

It turned out to be a beautiful morning for Sarah and Heather. A complete denial of the events from yesterday. They both took their time getting ready, Sarah because she just didn't feel like rushing and Heather because she felt incapable of rushing. It had only been three beers, but she still woke up with a bit of a headache. Sarah had suggested that she might be dehydrated and should drink several glasses of water. Heather's head recommended that she drink several glasses of scotch. She did neither, taking two aspirin with a cup of coffee.

On their drive in, Heather wondered aloud what the day might be like.

"I wonder if we'll have a rush today like we did yesterday?"

Sarah said, "I doubt it. So many things happened, so many things …" Her voice trailed off.

Heather started feeling a little nervous about where Sarah's mind was going so decided to change the subject, "So, Sarah, you're getting your car worked on over at Pep Boys this morning?"

Sarah moved like she had just woken from a daydream, "Yes, yes, I am. Jimmy was able to get the parts over in Amarillo. They were back-ordered, so it took longer than expected. He also said there might be other work needed later but the rings will cure any short-term concerns." She smiled at Heather, "It's going to take all day, from what he told me. But, don't worry, I've got a car reserved over at Hot Poppers Car Rental. The walk isn't all that long. So, after that I'll pick you up. You know, at the correct time, of course."

Heather smiled, "Okay, that's great. Well, looks like we're here. Good luck with your car."

Sarah watched Heather exit the car with a wave. She waved back. *Such a lovely girl.*

* * *

After dropping off the car and alleviating Jimmy Johannsen's concern about the cost, she finished arranging the car rental. Sarah didn't care how much the repairs would be; she was going to keep her grandparents' car running no matter what.

She ended up renting a 5-year-old Corolla. It was a nice automobile, although smaller than her grandparents' Bel Air. Once she had figured out all the modern conveniences, which took a half-hour out of her day, she felt confident enough to drive over to the Antelope Valley Police Station. She parked in front and then proceeded through the front office door. She was met by a receptionist working the front desk. The receptionist's badge indicated she was also the police dispatcher.

"Can I help you, ma'am?"

"Yes, my name is Sarah Bennington. I would like to speak to Officer Stoner, please."

"About?"

"It's a personal matter."

"I understand. Let me see if he's in back."

The receptionist, Nelda, walked back by the officer desks. She saw Mike Glatt but no Mark Stoner. Glatt looked up as she approached.

"Hey, Nelda, what's up?"

"There's an elderly woman at the front, looking for Mark. Says her name is Sarah Bennington."

"Oh, well, maybe I can help. She was one of the people Poltroon took a shot at yesterday."

"Holy Cow! That's her!?"

"Yep. Let's go out front and see what she wants."

After they both appeared, Glatt introduced himself. Sarah asked, "Mark isn't here?"

Glatt replied, "Mark is out helping corral a delinquent cow."

Sarah smiled, "Do you know when he'll be back?"

Glatt said, "Not exactly … Is it something I can help you with?"

"I don't think so. I need … um, some DNA testing done. Since Mark helped Heather with that, I thought that maybe he could suggest …"

Glatt interrupted, "Actually, I was the one involved in the DNA testing part."

"Oh, well, uh, okay, I have two samples. I need to have tests done to see if they are related. How do I do that?"

Glatt smiled, "I can definitely help you with that. My uncle is Medical Director of the laboratory over at the Medical Center. Here's what you need to do. I'll make a call and let them know that you'll be coming over. There will be paperwork for you to fill out. After completing it, you will turn over the samples to them and then they'll take care of it. Just so you know, this is not the kind of thing covered by insurance. It'll be costly."

It was Sarah's turn to smile, "Oh, I don't care how much it costs. I just want to make sure I get correct results."

Glatt nodded, "You'll be in good hands. They're top notch over there. Go ahead and drive over, I'll call ahead for you."

"Thank you so much, Officer Glatt. I appreciate it."

"No worries at all Ms. Bennington, have a nice day."

He watched the lady leave and get in her car. He picked up the front desk phone and punched in the direct line to the laboratory. While he waited for them to pick up, Nelda said,

"Kind of weird, huh?"

"Not as weird as yesterday. Wait, it was as weird as yesterday, just not as exciting … WELL HELLO, Gertrude, Mike here. Yes, I'm fine. How are you?" Before she could answer the question in her typical five-minute monologue, he added, "Say, the reason I called is, there's a nice lady headed your way by the name of Sarah Bennington. What? Yes, *that* Sarah Bennington. She needs to have DNA tests for genetic comparison done. No, I don't know why and it doesn't matter … *does* it? Okay, then. Take care of her, all right? Good deal, thanks, Gertrude … mm hm, bye."

After hanging up Mike Glatt sighed, turned to Nelda and said, "Gertrude is a sweetie, but boy is she a snoop."

* * *

Glatt was at his desk for only fifteen minutes when he heard Nelda shout from the front desk,

"Is Mark back yet?"

Glatt got up. Did Sarah Bennington run into an issue? When he arrived at the front desk, he saw that it was Mark's uncle, Frank Peterson.

"Oh, hi, Frank. Mark's not back yet. He's out chasing a cow. Are you here to speak to your … *client*?"

Frank Peterson chuckled then said, "Yes, he in back?"

"Yep," said Glatt, lifting the hinged countertop to let the attorney pass through.

As they walked toward the holding cell, Glatt said, "We'll set you up in the Interview Room."

Frank Peterson nodded, "Does he know I'm going to represent him?"

Glatt replied, "Actually not yet. Mark intended to let him know but got called out. I think he planned on mentioning it when he got back. Guess it's taking longer than he anticipated."

"It's okay, not a big deal."

When they arrived at the holding cell, they saw the remains of a breakfast tray that Joss had left on the floor and the party of interest in a sitting position on the bed with his legs up and his hands casually placed behind his head.

Glatt pulled out the key to unlock the cell, "Joss, your lawyer is here."

Joss frowned, "This some kinda joke?"

Glatt and Peterson looked at each other and then back at Joss.

Peterson said, "No, I'm going to represent you … with your permission of course."

"Someone from Stoney's family representin' me. Ya'll think I cain't smell a setup? I weren't born yesterday."

Peterson sighed, "Mr. Poltroon, the court can assign you a public defender if that's your preference."

Joss thought for a moment, "I cain't afford you."

"Mr. Poltroon, I'm handling your case pro-bono. That means you won't be paying me anything."

Joss looked confused, "This all sounds kinda fishy ta me."

"Mr. Poltroon, let's have a private discussion. If after that, you still don't want to move forward, I'll personally petition the court to assign a public defender. That will take some time and you will be confined here until then. Right now, I can work to move up your arraignment and make arrangements for bail."

Suddenly the idea of a discussion didn't sound so bad to Joss. He didn't know what game Stoner might be playing, but it couldn't hurt to hear this man out. Even he had heard about Peterson's reputation. He was indeed a good lawyer.

When they were in the interview room, Frank Peterson looked Joss in the eye, "I want you to know that this is a serious situation. You could potentially be charged with attempted murder."

Joss was enraged, "For a fuckin' illegal wetback!? Are you fuckin' kiddin' me? They're comin' over the border. Tearin' this country apart is what they're doin'. I'm a goddam pa-truht. They should be givin' me a medal."

Frank Peterson tried hard not to shake his head, "Look, you came into the Elkhorn Café with a loaded weapon. It discharged, and thank god, no one was hit by the bullet."

Joss shrugged and mumbled, "Well …"

Peterson was already starting to regret representing this guy, "This is no time to be insouciant, Joss."

'Inn .. soo .. what?"

Peterson sighed, "Insouciant, it means showing a lack of caring."

Joss nodded his affirmation. "So what? I'm being arrested for trying to protect our country. They should be givin' me a medal. That beaner shouldn'a been here. Them illegals come …"

Peterson had just about enough of this idiot, "Shut up for a second. That 'beaner' is a U.S. citizen. Not only that, he's worked for years for the IRS in Washington, DC."

"Well, then, it wuz an honest mistake, I mean…"

"Knock it off, Joss! You're going to land your ass in jail and serve hard time with that mouth of yours."

"Okay, okay, whaddya want me to do?"

"For starters, shut your yap and listen. In court, here's what you're going to say. You were walking down the sidewalk with the intent of going to the gun shop two blocks down when you spotted what you thought were some friends. You decided you would go in and ask them to wait while you visited the gun shop to have your rifle looked at. You forgot to unload the rifle. Think you can remember that?"

Joss reluctantly nodded, "Shouldn' hafta, but yeah … I got it."

Peterson finally felt like he had made some progress, "Okay, I'm going to go see what arraignment date we can get and also if we can get a decent plea out of the DA. In the meantime, you say nothing to anyone. Understand?"

Peterson rose and walked to the door, but looked at Joss before turning the doorknob, "Nothing to no one." He opened the door and called out, "Mike? We're done here for now."

Glatt walked back from his desk to the room and escorted Joss to the holding cell after saying a 'so long' to the attorney. After locking the cell door, he asked Joss, "So, how did it go?"

"Nothin' to no one."

CHAPTER TWENTY-NINE

Mark had decided to swing by the Elkhorn after finally corralling Mrs. Riley's cow back into her field. This time he pleaded for her to fix the fence that she was supposed to have taken care of the last time he had been called out. He watched her nod her *almost* sincere agreement. *Yeah, right ... we'll see.*

Mark parked the cruiser and halted as soon as he entered the front door. His father was talking with Mr. Porter and they were both staring at the wall by the jukebox. It was where Mark had made an impression of Joss Poltroon.

"Dad, you don't need to have Mr. Porter fix that. I can spackle and paint that."

"Nobody is to touch it, Son."

"Huh? What do you mean?"

"Mr. Porter is going to make a sign for me."

"A sign…"

"Yep, it's gonna read, THIS IS WHAT HAPPENED TO THE LAST GUY THAT BROUGHT A LOADED WEAPON INTO OUR CAFÉ."

"Please don't do that."

"Already done. You're just gonna hafta deal with it."

With that comment, Mark's dad turned to walk back to the kitchen and Mr. Porter put away his little pencil and pocket notepad and exited the café giving Mark a pat on the shoulder as he passed.

Mark saw Heather by the counter. With his hat in hand, he focused his puzzled look at her and pointed at the wall. *Why is he doing this?*

Heather shrugged back. *Beats me.*

Mark walked over to Heather, "Can I talk to you in back?"

"Sure."

When they started to go into the office, Mark asked Mabel, "Mom, can Heather and I have a private moment in the office?"

"Okay, son," said Mabel giving Ed an elbowed nudge.

"Leave 'em alone, Mabel," admonished Ed.

"I didn't do nothin', I didn't say nothin'," complained Mabel.

After shutting the door and sitting his hat on door's coat hook, Mark turned to Heather.

Heather asked, "What did you want to ta …."

Mark grabbed her and kissed her so passionately that he nearly doubled her over backwards.

Heather gasped, "Wait, wait, I need a breath."

Mark said, "Sorry, I just couldn't wai …"

Heather jumped on Mark kissing him with her arms around his neck and her legs wrapped around his hips, knocking him back onto the desk. The stapler hit the floor, the lamp fell on top of the chair adjacent to the desk and two three-ring binders toppled from the book shelf. The commotion did not go unnoticed.

Mabel spun around at the sound, "What are they *doing* in there!"

Ed smiled and said, "They're havin' a private discussion."

It was a few moments later that Heather emerged, straightening her apron. Several rogue locks of hair had tried to escape the confines of hair clips and she was glowing a bright pink.

Mark followed with his tie crooked, a loop of it hanging above the loosely attached tie clip, his utility belt askew and lipstick smears on the side of his mouth which he was trying desperately to wipe away with a tissue.

Mabel followed the parade with wide eyes, "I guess it was a serious one."

Ed smiled again, "Yep. Well, let's get ready for the lunch crowd. After yesterday, I don't want to be caught with my … apron down." He chuckled. Mabel rolled her eyes while she wrung out the wash cloth before walking over to wipe down table six.

* * *

Sarah finally found the lab after meandering around the medical center for a few minutes. The various departments and offices were arranged in a square pattern on each floor. The departmental signs mounted beside the front door to each were plastic squares ten inches to a side. If you were unfamiliar with the facility and walking fast, you could pass right by without seeing them.

She entered through the main door and found a aisleway to her left which terminated at a desk occupied by a middle-aged receptionist. According to the desk plate, her name was Gertrude.

Sarah cleared her throat, "Excuse me, but I'm here to get a DNA test done. I believe officer Mike Glatt called and said to expect me?"

The woman looked up, "Oh, yes, Ms. Bennington. Mike called. Such a nice young man. He said you would be stopping by. I've got all the paperwork lined up for you. If you'll take the seat here next to the desk, I'll walk you through it."

Sarah sat down clutching her purse. She tried to appear calm, but her white knuckles were giving her away.

* * *

Mike Ahmadi had arrived to work a bit early. He had made the decision but somehow it still gnawed at him. *Has my life been a lie? Why would my father perpetrate a ruse? My mother never let on about anything. I was always her son.* Then the other problem invaded his mind, *What in the world will I do if it turns out we are NOT related? The woman tried to jump in front of a bullet on my behalf. How will I explain to her that she is mistaken?*

He knew that fretting would accomplish nothing. There was no path to follow that didn't involve first knowing the truth. And he would have to rely on science for that. His thoughts were interrupted by his desk phone ringing.

He picked up the receiver, "Hello, Mike Ahmadi."

"Mike," it was Salman, his supervisor, "welcome back from your trip. Can you swing by my desk and get me caught up on your progress with the tax report? Thanks."

Before he could answer, he heard the connection go dead. He hung up the phone. Well, he couldn't blame his supervisor. Salman had been under a lot of pressure recently with all of the changes the administration wanted to implement. Mike could at least lighten his concern a little bit. He had completed the report ahead of time since he wasn't sure what impact his trip would have on his schedule. He unlocked his desk file drawer and retrieved the half-inch thick manila folder.

Salman's door was open. Mike reached in and gave a tap on it, "Hey, Salman, is now, okay?"

Salman Kudu pushed the three-ring binder closed that he had been perusing and waved him in,

"Absolutely. How was your trip?" This time he waited for an answer.

"It was … interesting."

"So, how are we doing? Will we have a report by the end of next week?"

"Actually … here," Ahmadi handed him the folder. "The first page is a summary of findings; the next four pages are high level representation of the analysis that was done. The rest is a detailed listing of anticipated cumulative payments to the Treasury broken out by industry, income strata and impacts to Federal Bank policies, etc. Of course, there's a lot more detail than I've stated but that's the gist."

Salman was impressed, *My golden goose has laid another precious egg.*

"Mike, that's terrific. Thank you."

"Salman, if you don't mind. I need to take a smoke break."

"Sure, that's fine. Thanks again for the early delivery on this. I won't forget it." Salman secretly celebrated the day that he had hired Ahmadi and was reminded frequently of what a good decision it was. *I will be riding along with you on your road to success.*

Balancing praise so you are happy but not so much that you will look for greener pastures. Then, with a shrug and a wry smile, he thought, *Such is my burden.*

Mike smiled and nodded. He didn't actually smoke. The 'smoke break' was their inside code for taking some time outside the building whether it was to grab a beverage, make a phone call or run a quick errand. This time it was to make a phone call. A call to his adopted brother Karam.

After exiting the lobby, Mike tapped the speed-dial number. He heard it ringing. A woman's voice answered. "May I speak to Karam Ahmadi, please. Yes, tell him it's Mike. Thank you." He waited for about thirty seconds and then heard the familiar voice.

"Brother! Why has it been so long? It's good to hear your voice."

"Likewise, Karam. I know it's been a while and I'm sorry that this isn't to catch up. I need your help with something."

"Hey, at least you called. So, what's going on? What do you need my help for?"

"Well, this will be a bit of a surprise, but I

need your assistance in getting help from your friend."

"Hmm, what friend?"

"The one that works in the genetics lab. The lab that does all the testing."

"Why on earth do you need that?"

"Well, …. that's a long story."

CHAPTER THIRTY

Things didn't move fast enough for anyone over the next two weeks. Joss was fuming because bail required collateral, so he was stuck. Still, he managed to stay silent. Heather and Mark's relationship had nearly reached the countdown to ignition. Sarah had waited on pins and needles for the DNA test results. The return of her grandparents' car was a welcome, if short lived diversion. Mike Ahmadi had waited hoping the results would come much later. A decision deferred was a decision he didn't have to make.

It was on the fifteenth day after submitting the samples that he arrived home and found an envelope waiting for him in his apartment mailbox. It was from the lab where he had sent the samples. He stared at the envelope as he walked to his apartment. After entering and locking the door, he placed the envelope on the dining table, walked to the bedroom and took off his jacket and shoes.

I'd better change clothes too. Get into something more comfortable. After hanging up his clothes and changing into a jogging suit, he walked back to the dining room table where he once again stared at the envelope. *Maybe I should make some tea first. Yes, that's a good idea.*

Mike stood in the kitchen sipping on his tea and had nearly downed half the cup when the angels on his shoulders appeared again. *Isn't this pointless? Will putting it off change the results of the test?* He sighed. *But waiting won't make the results any different either, so what's the harm?*

He mumbled, "I'm being ridiculous." He sat the cup down in the sink and walked over to the dining table, pulled out a chair, sat down, and tapped the envelope's contents to one end. He tore off the opposing end, blew the envelope open and took out the three pages of results. The first page basically gave him the percentage match between the two samples and the likelihood of familial match. His eyes bugged out. He looked at the clock. He might still be able to catch the analyst who had done the workup. The performing tech area of the report showed a signed name of Jasmina H.

He grabbed his cellphone and dialed the number printed on the header. He heard the phone ringing. A man's voice picked up. "Hello, Genetics Lab, Carlos speaking."

"Um, yes, this is Mike Ahmadi. I just had DNA matching tests done by your lab. It says it was done by someone named Jasmina. Is it possible to speak with her about the report?"

"Let me check and see if she's still here."

Ahmadi found himself hoping it was some kind of mistake. *Maybe somehow it will turn out to be clerical or some oth ...*

"Hello, this is Jasmina. Who am I speaking to?"

"Oh, this is Mike Ahmadi. I just got some results that, well, uh, surprised me. You were the analyst and I was hoping to discuss it with you."

"I was on my way home. Can this wait until tomorrow?"

"Well, it's very important to me. I only have one question basically."

"Okay, what is it?"

"Are you sure the results are correct?"

Jasmina looked at the phone receiver as if she were talking to an extraterrestrial, "Of *course* the results are correct. We don't release incorrect results."

"I didn't mean to offend you. It's just that it's a bit of a shock and I was wondering if, you know, the possibility, that something might have, well, been overlooked or something might …"

"Look, we run everything in duplicate." Then she sighed, "What are the test order numbers?"

"Excuse me?"

"The emboldened number printed on the upper left of the second page."

Ahmadi turned the first page over, "It's TS-5009623 and below that TS-5009624."

"Okay, give me a sec' here."

Ahmadi could hear the click of computer keys. Then she came back on the phone.

"Okay, I've got the data that you're looking at. Oh yeah, the two are most definitely related."

"How can you be so sure of that?"

"Mitochondria."

"Mitochondria?"

"Yes, they're the batteries of the cell that produces energy to …"

Ahmadi interrupted, "Yes, yes, I remember that from biology class. So, what about mitochondria?"

"A person's mitochondria can only come from their mother."

"What!? Are you sure?"

Jasmina replied, "Quite sure. You can look it up." For several seconds she heard nothing but silence from the other end. "Hello?"

"Yeah, yeah, I'm here," Ahmadi replied tersely.

"Oh, I'm sorry. I didn't mean to seem insensitive. Apparently, you weren't expecting the woman's sample to show she was related to your ... other sample?"

"Uh, sorry, I've got to go." Ahmadi quickly disconnected the call.

"Mr. Ahmadi, I ..." It was too late. Jasmina was listening to dial tone.

Ahmadi's mind was tumbling. His life in Afghanistan had been based on a lie. *Well, if not an outright lie, certainly subterfuge.* He tried to calm down by slowing his breathing. *If I had been in my father's shoes, what would I have done? Would I have kept the knowledge of who my birth mother really was a secret?* He had to admit that he probably would. But as much as he tried to ally the facts with loyalty to his father, one stubbornly refused. He lowered his head. *I could not have abandoned the mother of my child.* Try as he might, he could not bring himself to find that acceptable, even if it was his father. He knew the man to be a leader that others looked up to. A man that was disciplined and proudly patriotic, but even so, he apparently had flaws. And now, Ahmadi realized he had a situation to deal with. *What should I do, now that I know the truth?*

* * *

Sarah had been getting more and more anxious. She started watching for the mail carrier's vehicle each day as it dropped off postal detritus in her mailbox. She would rush out as soon as the mail carrier drove off to check the contents. Day after day, there was nothing but ads with the exception of the gas, electric and phone bills. Heather had debated with Sarah over the need for two phones but Sarah couldn't let go of the old-style rotary phone hanging on the wall by the kitchen doorway. It was the size of a wall clock but Sarah had too many memories tied up in that device to let it go.

It's been two weeks. Why is it taking this long? Sarah sat at the end of the couch and stared out the window, wondering if the mail would finally relinquish the results she was hoping for.

As if by invocation, the mail van pulled up by her mailbox. Unlike the other days, the mail carrier gave the horn two short beeps as they drove away. *Is that an omen?*

Sarah hustled off the couch and left the house doing her version of a speed walk. Once again, a heart sinking emotion arose as the opened mail box seemed to contain only flyers for the grocery store in town. As they were pulled from the box, an envelope dropped to the ground. Sarah bent over and picked it up. She turned it over and saw that it was addressed to her and had the return address for Antelope Valley Medical Center. Immediately following on the next line was the word ***Laboratory***, with the street address and zip code completing the sender's identity.

She was momentarily stymied by the urge to

rush into her house to read it while wanting to put off knowing the contents a bit longer. Sarah suddenly had a pair of angels of her own on her shoulders. *You're being silly Sarah; you know it's your son. It has to be. But what if he isn't. Are you prepared to discover that? Nothing ventured, nothing gained. But, ignorance IS bliss.*

She hadn't really considered the possibility of Mike Ahmadi not being Joseph. *Have you let zealousness overshadow reason? Everything is pointing toward him being your boy. Maybe God is toying with you yet again; have you considered that?*

"Oh, shut up! Both of you!" Sarah looked around. There was no one anywhere to witness her outburst. She was grateful for that. *I'll just walk normally back to the house and find out what this says.* She once again began a speed walk, but this time it was unintentional.

* * *

Frank Peterson appeared at the front desk of the police station with a grim look on his face. This time Nelda informed him that Mark was in back as well as the captain. Mike Glatt had called in sick.

"That's okay," replied the attorney, "I'm here to talk with my client."

"Okay, come on in back. I'm sure Mark can help you out."

When Peterson walked through the doorway to the back, Mark looked up to see his uncle's approach.

"Hey, Uncle Frank. Here to talk to Joss?"

"Yep."

Mark noticed that his uncle didn't seem to be in a good mood.

After getting Joss and Frank settled in the interview room he said, "If you need anything, let me know." He was looking at his uncle.

Joss spoke up, "Yeah, get me a soda."

Mark replied pointing, "The water cooler's in the corner."

Mark shut the door and walked back to his desk.

Joss let out a, "Pffft." He looked at his attorney and asked, "So when do I get to tell my side of the story and go home? I'm sick and tired of bein' in here."

Once again, Joss had managed to make his attorney incredulous, "You aren't going to testify."

"Whadja mean? I was helping to protect my country, my town. I …"

"Just shut up. There's been a development."

"What kinda development?"

Leaning in and staring Joss in the eye, "Did you say anything out loud before you took that rifle into the café?"

Joss leaned back, "Um, I dunno, maybe, I guess."

"Well, there were two townsfolk behind you and they heard your yapping as they passed."

"Okay, so what?"

"It's enough that the District Attorney is thinking strongly of charging you with a hate crime."

"I dunno whut that means."

"It means that if they push forward and you're convicted, you will go to federal prison. Because you used a gun to intimidate, let alone intend to cause bodily harm, you can get anywhere from one to ten years in prison AND potentially pay a fine."

Joss was speechless.

"There! That right there!" said Peterson. "That's all I want to ever see or hear from you here on out. Now, I think I can shake up the credibility of the witnesses' statements. If I can convince the D.A. that he'll risk a loss, and that you'll accept a deal, then we can try to get a plea agreement for minimal jail time and keep any fines small. But, if you open your mouth to even sneeze, I'll drop your case like a hot potato and you can take your chances with a Public Defender or hire another lawyer. Got it?"

After a long pause, Joss mumbled, "Nothin' ta no one."

As Peterson got up to leave, he said, "Not even *that* much."

* * *

Sarah entered through the front door, and after closing it, proceeded to the dining room where she laid the envelope on the table. Heather was at work at the café, so Sarah wouldn't have to leave to pick her up for another two hours. She paused to look at it and then decided to use the restroom.

After washing her hands, she exited the bathroom and from the kitchen doorway stared once again at the envelope resting on the dining room table.

She muttered to herself, "You know, I could really go for a cup of coffee right now."

Sarah placed a makeshift paper towel filter in the basket and added fresh coffee grounds. She filled the pot with water and then carefully placed the glass bulbed lid over the assembly and positioned the pot in the center of the stove. Like a hundred other times, she took a match from the holder, struck it, and then held it by the burner as she turned on the gas. With the familiar 'whoof' of ignition, it came to life. Sarah moved the coffee pot onto the burner. Now she had ten to fifteen minutes of antsy wait time before it would be ready. Her nerves, along with the angels on her shoulders, began their harassment again. *Why not sit down and open the letter while the coffee perks? You'll feel better having a nice cup of coffee while you review the results. You know you want to see what it says! Rushing now will not change the results!*

She had spent about nine minutes playing tennis in her mind with the battling between 'read it now' and 'don't read it now'- back and forth, back and forth. Her nervousness finally moved her to action. She left the kitchen and pulled up a chair by the dining room table. She ripped open the envelope. There were three pages.

She turned the introductory page immediately and looked at the second page. It had order numbers for each specimen. This was followed by a bunch of technical stuff she didn't really understand. She moved on to page three. It displayed more technical stuff on the top half followed by a signature, date, lab name and address where the testing had been performed.

How is this helpful? Does everyone have to get a degree in Biology to read this stuff? Sarah turned over the pages and placed the report out flat on the table. That's when she saw it. It was right after the salutation. In her haste, she had blown right past it.

DNA Test Result: DNA comparison between samples, one male, one female, shows that the probability of maternity is 99.985%.

Sarah gasped. She didn't realize she had stopped breathing. She read it over and over. It seemed to shock her but then she thought, *Why am I shocked when it's something I knew in my heart?* It even seemed to have affected her sense of smell. It was some kind of burnt smell. This was followed by the sound of hissing.

"Oh no, the coffee!"

She ran into the kitchen and saw that the pot had boiled over onto the stove-top. Her nose was assaulted by the strong odor of burnt coffee. *No, cremated*, she thought.

She removed the coffee pot from the stove while she turned the burner off with her left hand. She placed the pot in the sink. Grabbing a few paper towels, she began wiping up the spillover and pondering what to do next.

Do I risk asking Mike Ahmadi about the results he got? Should I wait and see if he contacts me? Oh dear, what if he refuses to accept the results? An ugly thought entered her mind. *What if he never had his samples tested? If I call him, will I know what to say? What if it upsets him and he turns his back? What if ...*

The smell in the kitchen started intruding into her thoughts. Sarah opened up the kitchen window.

The air that entered never smelled so good. She emptied the coffee pot, took out the brew basket and dumped the ruined contents into the kitchen trash can. After rinsing and refilling the pot, she returned it to the stove, and once again, lit the burner.

Talking to herself, she said, "There, a fresh start." Her own comment gave her pause. *A fresh start to ... what?*

CHAPTER THIRTY-ONE

Mike Ahmadi wrestled with the new-found information. Should he contact Sarah Bennington? *Perhaps I should call her on the phone? No, you'll probably get all tongue tied and say the wrong thing. What to do, what to do?*

The more he thought about it, the more sense it made that he write down his thoughts. That way he could review it later and see if it communicated what he wanted to say. *Do I even KNOW what I want to say?* Still, it seemed to him to be the best approach.

He started writing down sentences. Some about his life in Afghanistan. Others chronicled his journey to get to America. *You idiot, you already told her a lot of that when you were with her.* He was a man of numbers but he eventually came to the conclusion that, sharing his emotions upon finding out this impossible news, meant a new start with this woman and something he felt ill-equipped to do. *Your mother*, he reminded himself. *She is obviously compassionate and therefore will understand why I want to proceed slowly.* It totally slipped past him that he had said 'proceed' in his thoughts.

Thanks to that police officer named Mark, Mike found out that the bullet that was fired in that cafe would have missed, even if he had been sitting up straight. But, he reminded himself, she did not know that at the time. It still amazed him that she tried to dive in front of a bullet for his sake. Although, given the DNA results, it now made a lot more sense. *She certainly deserves my respect and appreciation, but how do I think about her as a mother at this point in my life? I've only known one mother up to now.*

He grabbed the tablet he had been using to construct a letter and struck through what he had written so far with his mechanical pencil.

"I need a fresh start." His comment gave him pause. *A fresh start to ... what?*

* * *

Sarah was feeling nervous and even though she would be too early to pick up Heather, she needed to do something other than hang around the house. She decided to drive into town.

When she arrived, she stopped by the café. Heather was wiping down a table. When she looked up and saw Sarah, she frowned. Turning to look at the wall clock, she saw that Sarah had arrived early. Really early.

Heather started to ask, "Sarah, why are ..."

Sarah raised her hand and said, "I just got fed up being at the house. Decided to come in early. I'm going to swing by the grocery store so thought I would ask if you need anything?"

Heather paused for a moment, "No-o-o ... nope, can't think of anything."

"Okay, then. Well, I'll be there if I'm not here when it's time to leave. If that's the case, just call the store."

"Got it." Heather looked at Sarah and added, "Are you doing okay? I mean, after all that's happened with ... you know."

"I think so. I'm not sure what's next and that makes me uncomfortable."

Heather raised her eyebrows, "That I DO know something about."

Sarah smiled gently, "Yes, you do, dear girl. Okay, then, I'm off and I'll ... see you after a bit?"

Heather winked and gave her a thumbs up.

Sarah left the café asking herself, *Why am I going to the grocery store?*

* * *

Heather had gone back into the kitchen to fetch a fresh wiping rag. When she came back out front, she saw Tim Harris looking at the wall depression and the sign hanging above it.

He turned his head when he noticed Heather walking toward him.

"Tim, how was your vacation? Did you enjoy your family reunion? Did you do anything exciting?"

"Not, apparently, as exciting as this," he said, pointing at the sign. "This is what happened to the last guy that brought a loaded weapon into our café? Care to fill me in?"

Heather relayed the story of Joss Poltroon and Mark's intervention. Tim started shaking his head.

"And to think I was at a stupid reunion when I could have been here to see this."

"Are you serious? You realize a bullet was fired."

"But you said no one was hurt."

Heather's facial expression conveyed, *Are you*

insane?

"Hey, don't look at me that way. This was Joss and Mark! Oh, how I would have loved to have seen that."

"Well, Tim, it scared the wits out of me. If it never happens again, it'll be too soon. Hey, what are doing here anyway? You're not due back for another three days."

"Thought I'd stop in and check on my hours. Just in case there were any changes."

"Well, Ed's in the kitchen and I'm sure he's gonna be glad to see that you're back."

"Thanks. So, anything new with you?"

"Well, things are starting to get serious with Mark."

This made Tim grin, "Starting? It's about frickin' time. You two were made for each other."

"Oh, I don't know. We like each other a lot but I'm not su ..."

"Oh my god, Heather. Take a clue! Everyone sees it!" Tim started walking toward the kitchen and with a wave of his arms added, "Women!"

* * *

Sarah parked in front of the supermarket. She waited a few seconds, trying to figure out if there's anything she could use as an excuse for being there instead of just killing time. Sighing, she gave up and exited her car.

After entering the store, she made a bee line to the meat department. A young man was behind the scale. "Can I help you, ma'am?"

"Oh, uh, is Henry Givens here today?"

"Just a moment. He's in back. I'll go get 'im."

"Thank you." As Sarah waited she looked around the store. She noticed a couple townsfolk were staring at her and whispering. When they noticed her looking they quickly turned away. This happened several times before she heard a familiar voice.

"Sarah, well finally. What can I do you for?"

"Hi, Henry. Well, I'm not sure. I, uh, I'm …"

"Hey, Sarah." The voice came from Sarah's right. It was Melinda Miller pushing a grocery cart toward her with Wayne in tow.

"Oh, hi, Melinda … Wayne."

Wayne responded with his usual, "Howdy."

Melinda leaned close to Sarah and whispered, "We heard the surprising news."

Sarah was momentarily stunned. *Did Donnie lie about telling anyone? I know Heather would never say anything.*

She cleared her throat and asked, "What news would that be?"

"You know, about the shooting at the café. And who was that strange young man that you seemed to know? No one around here has ever heard of him."

"Someone from my past."

"Well, some in town are gossipin' about it bein' ... more than an acquaintance."

"What do you mean?" asked Sarah.

Melinda raised an eyebrow, "Surely you realize the two of ya look sorta alike."

Sarah started to blush and whispered, "Melinda, I really don't want to talk about this!"

"I just wanted ya to know that I'm happy for you if it's ... you know ... and to let you know that folks are talkin'."

Wayne, who had been silent until now said

loudly, "Folks should mind their own damn business!"

"Wayne Miller!" admonished Melinda, "Watch your language!"

"Needed sayin'."

In spite of everything, Sarah smiled, "Thank you, Wayne. I …"

"Is this your local hangout or are you folks gonna want somethin'?" It was Henry Givens, waiting patiently by the scale.

Sarah turned, "Yes, Henry, thank you. Hmm … I'd like two pounds of thick sliced bologna in two one-pound packages. Thank you."

"Comin' right up."

After getting the paper wrapped deli meat, Sarah handed one to Melinda.

"Here you go. My treat." Smiling, she added, "Something for you to feed the folks that are talkin'."

Wayne snickered, "Baloney for all the baloney."

Melinda swatted his arm, but as she turned to walk away, she winked at Sarah with a little smile on her face.

Sarah smiled back at Melinda but she hoped folks didn't know that the gossip wasn't baloney. She also didn't know why she expected to keep it a secret, nor WHY she would want to keep it a secret. *After all this time, why would the opinions of the Antelope Valley citizens matter to me? Maybe it's true that you can take the girl out of the small town but not the small town out of the girl.*

Sarah brought herself back from her introspection and stared at the paper wrapped bologna she still held in her hand. Not knowing what else to do, she took the lunch meat she didn't really need to the front register, and after paying for it, went and sat in her car for a few moments to ponder what she would say to Heather about her purchase. Looking at the shopping bag's contents in the seat next to her, she thought, *Looks like I'm the one that's full of baloney.*

CHAPTER THIRTY-TWO

Mike Ahmadi once again tore a page from the paper pad, wadded it, and threw it on the floor. Sighing, he arched his back to relieve some of the strain. He looked down and saw that he had carpet bombed his floor with paper balls. *Might as well take a break and clean this up.*

After the plastic kitchen-sized trash sack had collected the detritus, he walked out to the garage and deposited the 'monument to his futility' into the garbage can.

As he walked back to the table to make yet another effort in writing to the woman he could no longer claim was not his mother, his cell phone vibrated on the table. The number and name indicated it was Karam.

Ahmadi picked up the phone, "Karam. What's up, brother?"

"Hey, Mike, I've got a bone to pick with you."

Ahmadi frowned, "Excuse Me? What are you talking about?"

"I heard that you were rude to Jasmina the other day. That's not like you!"

It was a good thing Karam couldn't see Mike blush, "Well, I wasn't exactly *rude*. I was terse, I guess and … yeah, I shouldn't have been. Hey, wait a minute. She complained to you about me?"

"No, no, her cousin told me. Apparently, they were chatting and she mentioned this rude guy who was questioning her work."

"Oh my gosh, that's overstating it. I was just verifying that the results were correct is all." After a moment, Mike asked, "You heard it from a cousin? Who's her cousin?"

"Salome."

"YOUR SALOME?"

"Yep, small world, huh? Anyway, I told Salome to tell Jasmina that the four of us would go out to dinner to make up for it. Your treat, of course. I'll call you back with the particulars."

"Wait, you little… ." It was too late, all Mike Ahmadi heard was a dial tone.

I've asked him to the point of exhaustion to stop setting me up with women and now he's done it again. And gotten a free meal out of it to boot! Well, at least he was right about one thing. It is indeed a small world.

*   *   *

Frank Peterson was grateful. He thanked his lucky stars that the District Attorney was new to the job. He was grateful that the current political climate made any jurors they could find within a 300-mile radius were politically right leaning toward the immigration problems at the southern border, never mind that the target had been a U.S. citizen of middle-east extraction. The DA caved and that is all that mattered. He would be free of the toadstool pro bono client his nephew had talked him into taking. It wasn't that he hated pro bono work, just that he preferred clients who paid, much, much more.

Glatt and Frank's nephew, Mark, were both at the station when the attorney arrived. It was Glatt that ushered him this time to the interview room. It was only a moment later that Joss Poltroon was escorted in.

Frank spoke first, "Have a seat, Joss. This will be quick."

"-K ," said Joss as he took a seat.

"I've worked out a deal with the DA. You'll

only have to serve six months in county jail and be on probation for two years. You'll need to make good on damages at the café but that turns out to be just a dented piece of metal and patching a couple of places where the bullet with through the ceiling and into the roof."

"Wait, why do I have to have any jail time? Somethin's not right."

Peterson had had enough, "Listen up. All the circumstances surrounding this have worked in your favor, not the least of which is having me as your attorney. You want to have a trial and spend two or more years in jail? Fine. I'll turn over my files to whoever you get as a public defender. Good luck with that; you'll need it." With that final comment, Peterson started to get up and leave.

"Aw right, aw right. Don't get your panties in a bunch. What's next?"

Peterson reviewed next steps with Poltroon and received confirmation to make the plea deal. Once their business was concluded, Frank started to leave but swung by his nephew's desk before heading out.

"Everything okay, Uncle Frank?" asked Mark.

"We need to have a chat later. I'll fill you in after the case is settled."

"Oh, okay."

Peterson turned and walked toward the exit leaving Mark to wonder about what there was to 'fill in' regarding Joss. It seemed straightforward. *Hmm, must be attorney-client privileged stuff. I guess I'll just have to wait.*

CHAPTER THIRTY-THREE

Karam had called Mike Ahmadi with the date and time for the dinner out 'with the girls' as he put it. *He made it sound like we're married couples. When is he going to finally give up?*

They would be meeting at the Chartreuse Griffin. It was a pricey restaurant. *Of course!* Mike had to admit that he loved the seafood there. The chowder was to die for. They baked their own sourdough rolls, served warm with butter, and the swordfish was heaven. At least he would have a very nice meal, even if it came with a small serving of crow to start. *I just hope this Jasmina doesn't turn out to be a sumo wrestler with coke bottle glasses.*

He arrived a few minutes early so decided to sit at their reserved table and wait for them there.

* * *

Karam had suggested to Salome and Jasmina that they share a taxi. It was a little crowded with the three of them but at least they didn't have to fight traffic and find a place to park. The valet charge at the restaurant was steep and besides, he didn't trust the valets with his new BMW. It was only a 320i but he had saved for four years for that sweet ride and he wasn't taking any unnecessary risks with it.

Jasmina, although she was already in the cab and on the way, once again voiced her objection to the extorted dinner that Karam and Salome had convinced her to attend.

"Karam, this really isn't necessary. You shouldn't have forced your brother into it."

"Ah, nonsense, he needs to purge his conscience." Turning sideways with a smile he added, "Or at least purge his wallet." He chuckled at his joke. Both Salome and Jasmina shook their heads.

Jasmina turned to Salome and asked, "What's he like?"

Salome said, "I don't know him all that well, but he's nice." Karam had to choke back a laugh. He covered his mouth with his hand and coughed. Mike wasn't her style of guy but she was impressed by his manners and intelligence on the few occasions they had met. She had mentioned this several times to Karam. They had also discussed finding a way for Jasmina and Mike to meet. Fortune had finally smiled.

Jasmina immediately thought, *Oh, dear. Nice. It's bad enough she keeps trying to set me up but now it's with someone who's ... nice.* She pictured a smiling sumo wrestler with coke bottle glasses.

A few seconds later, it was Karam who said, "Well, we're here." He felt his phone vibrate. Taking it from his coat pocket, he saw that he had a text from Mike. Reading it, he said, "Okay, Mike's inside. He's got our table. Let's exit this buggy and head on in."

One by one they extricated themselves from the taxi. Karam paid the cabbie and after pocketing his wallet, joined the ladies at the restaurant entrance. The door was opened by a restaurant employee.

"Welcome to the Chartreuse Griffin."

*   *   *

Mike Ahmadi knew that he probably should have waited, but he had been in this situation before, so he ordered a glass of red wine right away. He had just taken his first sip when he noticed a woman walking by. She was tall and slender. Her brunette hair was up with a braided bun in the back held in place by two colorful chopsticks. The sleeveless dress was a shimmering silver brocade that fit her figure.

The shawl that draped both arms and the small of her back looked to be made of the same material. Her black onyx necklace and earrings closely matched her clutch purse and shoes.

Mike never took his eyes off her as she passed, *Now, why couldn't THAT be Jasmina?*

* * *

Jasmina had gotten a little separated from Karam and Salome in the busy restaurant. She didn't realize that they had been delayed and were now trailing quite a bit behind her. She noticed the handsome man sitting at the table staring at her. As she passed, he looked away to his left.

She thought, *Now, why couldn't THAT be his brother?*

* * *

Mike caught sight of Karam and Salome. He frowned, confused. *What? No Jasmina?*

Karam felt like he and Salome were running an obstacle course. Looking around, he spotted Mike. He waved and Mike returned the salutation. Karam started making his way toward the table holding Salome's hand. Karam turned to Salome.

"Where's Jasmina?"

Salome said, "She must not have realized we got stalled behind her by the large party we ran into." Salome continued to scan the restaurant as they walked toward Mike, "There she is!"

Karam gave a large wave. Jasmina smiled as she saw it.

Mike couldn't see who he was waving to. Four gentlemen were getting ready to take their chairs at the next table. Mike briefly rose and then sat back down as Salome and his brother arrived at the table. As they took their seats, Salome greeted Mike.

"Hi, Mike. Boy, busy night at the restaurant, huh?"

Mike raised an eyebrow, "Yeah, it really seems to be hoppin'. So, did Jasmina back out on dinner?"

Karam frowned, "Naw, she's here. She was in front of us. Surprised you didn't see her."

Mike sighed, "I've … never … met … her."

Karam shrugged, "Yeah, right. My bad. Oh, here she is now."

Mike turned to his right in the direction his

brother was looking and the stunning woman in the brocade dress approached and stood next to the remaining chair at their table.

Karam pointed with his outstretched hand, "Mike, I'd like you to meet Jasmina. Jasmina, this is my brother, Mike Ahmadi."

Mike realized that he was staring with his mouth agape. He snapped it shut then said in a rush, "Oh, um, uh, here, let me get your chair for you." As he hurriedly rose, he banged his right knee cap against the heavy oak table's leg.

"Son of a …"

Oh my god, it's HIM! Jasmina asked, "Are you all right?"

Mike hobbled a bit as he pulled out her chair, "Yes, I'm okay, I'm fine … I think."

Jasmina felt nervous but reminded herself that she could remain calm and professional if she just concentrated. As Ahmadi tried to push in her chair, she had also tried to move her chair and the sudden rush made her take a firm grip of the chair's arms. In order to do this, she had to abandon her clutch purse which fell forward onto the table perfectly striking the upcurved handle of a dining fork. It went into the air performing a triple somersault before clanking on the tile floor.

Mike bent over mumbling, "I can get that."

Jasmina didn't hear him. Totally chagrined, she hurriedly bent sideways in her chair to pick up the embarrassing implement. Both of them would later swear that the collision had made a physical noise.

Mike was sitting on the floor holding his head and Jasmina was leaning forward with her elbows on the table doing the same. He picked himself up after a few seconds and took his seat. Jasmina leaned back in her chair. They both spoke in synchrony.

"I'm so sorry."
"I'm so sorry."

With a small smile, Mike added, "Perhaps we should call it a draw." The comment made Jasmina smile. *My god, even her smile is beautiful.*

"I'm fortunate to have been blessed with a hard head."

"Well, you've certainly been blessed with a beautiful one." *Oh crap, I said that out loud.* Even with her flawless light brown complexion, Mike could tell she was now blushing.

"My apologies, I didn't mean to embarrass you."

"It's all right. A lady doesn't mind compliments from a handsome gentleman." It was now Mike's turn to blush as he returned to his seat.

Karam was getting a sore neck looking back and forth at these two. *Who the hell are these people and what did they do with my friend and my brother?*

Karam sighed and said, "Well, now that *INTRODUCTIONS* have been made, shall we order dinner?"

CHAPTER THIRTY-FOUR

Dinner had been eaten but hardly tasted. To both Mike and Jasmina, it seemed as though they had known the other for years. They found each other easy to talk to. They shared so much in terms of music, art, the conciseness with which they each approached their work.

They were so wrapped up in each other, no notice had been given to the ring on Salome's finger. Karam had to shake them out of their reverie.

"Hey!"

Mike came up with a start, "What?"

"I'm trying to share something with you two."

"Oh, okay, sorry, what is it?"

Jasmina actually knew already. If there's anything a woman notices, it's when a new engagement ring is on the finger of another. Jasmina had to begrudgingly admit that she was jealous of Salome. She surreptitiously looked at the third finger of her own left hand.

"I've asked Salome to marry me and she said yes!"

Mike clapped Karam on the shoulder,

"Wonderful! Congratulations! I'm happy for you both. Show us the ring!"

Salome held out her hand. Jasmina and Mike both gave accolades. Salome beamed. It was a few moments later that her expression turned to concern. She grabbed Karam's arm.

"I need the ladies room. Now!"

Karam jumped up, held Salome by the elbow and ran interference for her through the restaurant.

Mike and Jasmina looked at each other, both hoping that it wasn't something she had eaten. Karam came back a couple of minutes later.

"She's okay. Just needed to throw up a little."

Mike asked, "Was it something she ate?"

Karam shook his head, "No, it wouldn't have mattered what she had eaten."

Mike looked puzzled and then his eyes popped, "Ohhhh."

Karam smiled, "Yep. Not exactly the *way* we had planned but it was part of the plan. It's only been four weeks and we didn't want to spring the news early."

Jasmina said, "I think I'll go check on her.

Just in case. Mike, it was very nice to meet you."

Mike frowned, "What are you talking about? I'm going to be right here until you get back."

Jasmina's heart fluttered a bit and she smiled, "Okay. I'll be just a minute."

When she smiled at him, he thought, *I'll DAMN sure be here when you get back.*

Karam saw the look on his brother's face, "Okay, so, what do you think?"

Mike replied, "About what?"

"Oh, give me a break! About Jasmina. She's something, huh?"

"Yeah, she's okay."

Karam snorted, "You are such a putz. In fact, I suspect you both are. If there were two people made for each other, not as much as Salome and myself mind you, it's you and Jasmina."

"All right, all right. Yeah, she's seems incredible. But, how do I know if she'll take an interest in me?"

"Were you even present when you two tried to merge brains?" He threw up his hands, "What does it take?"

Mike had to grin. His brother could be hilarious even when he was trying to be serious.

"Look, Karam, I'm definitely going to do everything I can to see her again. Is that good enough for now?"

Karam shrugged, "Eh, for now, I guess."

A peaked Salome appeared, being escorted by Jasmina. She paused at the table to take a few deep breaths.

"Karam, sweetie, I think I need to go home. I'm sorry."

"It's not a problem. I'll get the Maitre D' to call a cab. Mike, Jasmina, sorry to break up the party early."

Mike had a thought, "You two go ahead. I'll take care of getting Jasmina home."

Jasmina paused, "Are you sure? I don't want to be any trouble."

Mike smiled, "You're not any trouble." Then frowning, he said, "Wait! You *aren't* trouble, are you?"

Jasmina covered her mouth with her hand as she laughed, "I try not to be."

Mike turned toward Salome, "Salome, get to feeling better. We'll do this again when you feel up to it." As they turned, he quickly added, "It'll be Karam's treat."

His brother looked over his shoulder and stared with squinty eyes and mouthed, *You little* ... . Mike couldn't make out the rest but he was sure it was insulting and totally appropriate.

He looked at Jasmina, who had returned to her seat, "Let's order a dessert to share."

CHAPTER THIRTY-FIVE

The ride home for Mike and Jasmina ended up being a continuum of their dinner conversation. There seemed to be an unending stream of things to chat about. Mike somehow managed to find a parking space near her apartment. They sat in the car and continued to talk. Time seemed to stand still.

Jasmina decided to ask Mike about the test, "You seemed a little upset when we talked about the test results during our phone call."

Mike paused and looked straight ahead. Jasmina was afraid that she had upset him again. He turned back to look at her.

"It was unexpected, is all. I'm embarrassed to think you felt I was taking it out on you."

Relieved, she said, "Oh, please don't be. Unexpected results can be upsetting. I'm just glad you're not mad at me."

Without thinking he took her left hand in his. He looked at the perfect brown skin, the pink nail polish on the delicate fingers. *She's ... she's ... words just fail.*

"That would be very difficult," he said

smiling, "More difficult than what I have to do."

Jasmina's smile turned into a slight frown. *Oh, dear, what is he going to say? I thought we were getting along so well.*

Mike continued, "The … woman…in question turns out to be my biological mother."

Jasmina's concern was replaced by surprise. She knew the samples were related but did not know the sources. That had been kept confidential … until now.

"I feel like I have to respond to her somehow but I don't think I have the words. I've lived thirty plus years understanding who and what I was only to find out that it wasn't true."

Jasmina took the hand holding hers and placed her right hand on top. She looked directly into Mike's eyes and said, "I know that when the time is right, you'll find the words." When she heard herself say the word time, something clicked. She looked at her watch. *Oh, my goodness!*

"Mike, I have to be to work in six hours. I hate to, but I need to go and get some sleep."

"Oh my gosh, Jasmina, of course. I've kept

you up. Wait, I'll get the door."

"You don't need to …" It was too late. Mike had already exited the car and was running around to open the door for her. He pulled open the passenger door and took her hand as she exited the vehicle.

"Thank you!"

"My pleasure." *And it IS my pleasure, lovely lady.*

He walked her to her door and waited while she fished out her keys. She turned to say good-night. Without thinking he took her gently in his arms and kissed her. Only afterward did he realize how forward he had been.

"Oh, Jasmina, I'm sorry, I don't, I wasn't, I …"

Jasmina smiled, "I'll let you get away with it this time. But … you'll have to pay a price."

Mike's left eyebrow raised, "Oh, really now. And what would that price be."

Jasmina touched her index finger to her chin and rocking slightly side to side replied.

"I think another evening out for dinner seems appropriate."

Mike shrugged and smiled, "I guess I have to face up to my punishment. I'll give you a call late tomorrow or the morning after and we can make plans."

"Sounds perfect." Jasmina unlocked her door and stepped inside, stopping by the doorframe.

"Good night, Mike."

"A very good night, Jasmina."

As Mike walked back toward his car, he thought, *A beautiful, smart woman who's dropped in my lap by my flake of a brother. What's the chance of that?*

After locking the door, Jasmina thought, *A handsome, well-mannered man who escorts me to my door. I thought no one did that anymore. AND he gets dropped into my lap by my cousin. What's the chance of that?*

* * *

Mark had been thinking about it for several weeks now but was too afraid to ask. The feelings he had toward Heather were so strong that he couldn't deny it even if he wanted to. *Why would I want to? What's wrong with you, all of a sudden you can't make a simple decision? But, what if she says no. The answer is automatically no if you never ask, dummy.*

Mike Glatt was watching Mark's catatonic state play out by the pencil that Mark was holding and watching it go back and forth like a metronome. Nelda entered the room and upon seeing Mark's expression, decided to check with Mike.

"Um, is he okay?"

"How can I tell?" snorted Glatt.

"Well, Frank Peterson is out front and wanted to have a word with Mark."

"Okay, send him back. I'll try to get our boy out of his trance."

Nelda headed back to the front and Mike Glatt started to break through Mark's rumination.

"Mark? … M-a-r-k? … MARK!"

Stoner jolted, looked up and said, "Wha?"

Your uncle's here and wants to chat."

"Oh, um, okay. Any idea why?"

"Nope, but here he is now. You can ask."

Frank Peterson walked towards Mark but stopped at Glatt's desk.

"Mike, we came to a plea agreement. Prisoner

Transportation Services will be moving Joss from here to the court holding cell pending formal arraignment and sentencing. The judge has agreed to the terms. He'll be serving six months over at County and then two-years of probation after that. Here's the number to save you a step. Can you call and coordinate with them?"

"Sure thing," said Glatt reaching for his phone.

"Uh, out front if you don't mind. I'd like a private chat with Mark."

That surprised Glatt. He looked back and forth between the two men, shrugged slightly, and said, "Okay ... I'll leave you to it."

After Glatt disappeared to the front office, Frank Peterson pulled up a chair beside Mark's desk.

Peterson paused then said, "I don't know if you heard what I told Mike."

"Yep, I caught most of it. I sort of predicted it when I first contacted you about the case."

"Did you predict how you might get your ass in a sling?"

Mark sat up straight, "What are you talking

about?"

Peterson leaned back in his chair, "Let's assume, hypothetically, that I had a client with an unexplained bruise on his temple. Now, it probably wouldn't impact his sentence but it would be part of a defense to, well, let's just say create some amount of doubt surrounding the chain of events. Who knows, maybe the cause of the bruise impacted my client's state of mind, assuming of course that it occurred in the initial sequence of events."

Mark cleared his throat and started to speak but Peterson held up his hand, "Now, if said bruise was induced by an officer, say, in subduing the suspect then I wouldn't have much leverage. But … ", Peterson paused for effect, "if the bruise occurred after the suspect was sufficiently subdued, it would be prudent to bring it up." With a wave of his hand, Peterson went on, "Having said all this, if I had managed to obtain a reduced plea deal for my hypothetical client, then it wouldn't benefit said client at all to introduce any doubt and might induce the D.A. to reconsider his position. It would definitely put the hypothetical officer's ass in a sling, though.

Do you get my drift?"

Mark nodded silently.

Peterson leaned forward and continued, "I would have reminded the hypothetical officer that the past is the past and regardless of the, again hypothetical, history between the arresting officer and defendant, I would suggest that he remember that he's a professional, that he recall his training and forget all the high school shit and focus on his future. Do you think the hypothetical officer would be capable of doing that?"

Mark paused a moment and then suddenly jumped from his chair, "He's going to do more than that. He's going to start right now."

Now it was Peterson's turn to be surprised. *What the hell?*

Mike Glatt had peeked around the corner to see if the two had finished just in time to see Frank Peterson lean in and say something which was followed by Mark jumping up and hastily leaving through the patrolmen's entrance.

Walking over to Peterson, Glatt said, "I got your client set up for transfer." After clearing his throat, he added, "What did you say to get our boy all spooked."

"I told him to focus on his future."

Glatt replied, "Huh … I'm guessing he took your advice?"

Peterson leaned back in his chair, "Yeah, sure seems like it." Looking at Glatt he said, "What's the chance of that?"

CHAPTER THIRTY-SIX

It turned out that Mike Ahmadi's efforts to write a letter to Sarah Bennington were failing. He couldn't bring himself to refer to her as *mother*, no matter the evidence. *How will I address her?* When he was contacted by Karam about another dinner out with the ladies, it was a welcomed interruption.

The only things that puzzled him about it was Karam appeared quite pleasant about dinner being 'on him' and after that keeping the dining location and name a secret. He didn't even share a street address. He emailed street by street turns with some distances on the final stretch. *Karam is up to something, I'm sure of it.*

Mike had called Jasmina the morning after their first date and almost every four hours thereafter. She had wondered if he would follow up the following day and got her answer much sooner than expected. It was a welcome surprise. By the time they arranged the date and time for the dinner, chatting with each other seemed like second nature to them both. Jasmina was curious about the circumstances when Mike told her.

"So, he didn't tell you *where* we would be having dinner?"

"Nope. He's up to something, though. The only thing he said was dress casual. He said it's not far from your place. So, pick you up around 7?"

"That's fine. If you don't know where we're having dinner, how will you know how to get there?"

"He sent me driving directions; street by street, turn by turn. Can you believe that?"

Jasmina giggled, "Oh my gosh, it's starting to sound like an adventure!"

Mike said, "Wel-l-l, we'll see about THAT." He paused, then added softly, "I'm really looking forward to seeing you again."

"Me too. Bye."

"Bye."

* * *

Jasmina must have been looking for him because as soon as Mike Ahmadi parked his car, Jasmina came rushing outside and around the vehicle. She opened the door and plopped into the passenger seat. She was wearing faded blue jeans with rolled up cuffs, bright floral print shirt with turned up collar and denim waist jacket with metal buttons. Her feet sported bright red converse sneakers. Her hair was up but with a pinned-up braid in the back.

My god, can she look any cuter?

Ahmadi smiled, "Well, you look ready for action."

Jasmina gave him an appraisal, "Hm, beige Dockers, blue long-sleeve button-collar shirt and buffalo-brown Sperry shoes. Are you sure you're not here to sell me a boat?"

Mike grinned, "Well, one of us may be over or under-dressed, but together we've got it covered."

Jasmina smiled, "Aye, aye, captain." She followed this with her musical giggle.

Mike couldn't help chuckling as he said, "Well, we're off … *matey*."

Mike handed the printout with Karam's directions to Jasmina and asked her to read them out loud as they progressed toward the target destination. When they arrived, Mike saw why Karam was not upset at having to buy dinner. They were staring at The Bonobo Blues food truck. In spite of the teal-colored anthropomorphic image splashed across the vehicle, it advertised 'Mexi-Cali' fusion cuisine. Mike wasn't sure what to expect since, based on the few times he had attended conferences in San Diego, he thought the cuisine was no different in California than it was in Baja, Mexico. One thing was certain. It was a damn sight cheaper than the Chartreuse Griffin.

Luckily, he found a parking space only a block away and as they approached the half dozen or so picnic tables and chairs, he spotted Karam and Salome. They had already grabbed a table.

Karam grinned ear to ear upon seeing Mike's expression.

"Now I know why you wouldn't tell me where we were going."

Karam stood up and shook his brother's hand, "I know, but trust me, the food here is terrific … if a bit eclectic. Hi, Jasmina."

"Hi, Karam. Hey, Salome, how are you doing?"

"I'm much better, thanks. I've been having some cravings, though."

Mike looked over at the food truck, "Well, this might be the right place for you then."

Karam said, "Why don't you gals chat while Mike and I go over and order some food. What would you like? Jasmina?"

Jasmina turned and looked at the menu painted on the sign next to the serving window, "Hmm, the cheeseburger burrito looks interesting. I'll try that … with fries and a coke."

"Salome?"

"Well, dear, my usual – the chicken quesadilla, with peanut butter, chunky if they have it, and dill pickle slices on the top … extra cheese. And I'd like a root beer."

Mike thought he heard his stomach gurgle upon hearing her food order but managed not to react. He nodded to Karam and they walked over to the ordering queue lined up in front of the window.

Karam asked, "So, how are things going with Jasmina?"

"My gosh, Karam, we just started dating!"

"Okay, fine, play coy. I could see the chemistry between you two in the first five minutes."

Mike acquiesced, "She's fantastic. I keep expecting a shoe to drop, you know, like maybe she has a prosthetic head or something but each time I see her …"

Karam almost laughed out loud, "Oh wow, but do you have it bad." Then he turned serious, "Listen, she is a great gal. Salome filled me in a little about her. She's been hurt before and if you think things aren't going to work out, you let her down gently, okay?"

"Karam, it's way too early for talk like that." He had to admit that he was understanding how it might have felt. If Jasmina dumped him now, even after such a short time, it would really sting. His heart was starting to glide down a giant slippery slide, picking up speed and he doubted he could slow it down or even want to. Nothing else was said for a minute or so.

"I wonder if love at first sight is real?" Mike hadn't meant to verbalize the thought.

Karam didn't notice it was an accident, "Yeah, yeah, I think it is. The real trick is to nurture it and not screw things up. Real love is a journey, a movement of life together. It's …"

"What can I get for you guys?" Karam was

interrupted by a big burly guy with rolled up sleeves and a stained apron that hung from his neck with long straps wrapped and tied around his waist.

Karam responded first, "Oh, I'd like the cheeseburger burrito, the usual way with a coke and chips. I also need a Salome Special but chunky peanut butter if you have it."

How long have Karam and Salome been coming here?

"And for you, buddy?"

Mike gave the man his last name and then, giving a quick glance at the menu, said "I need a cheeseburger burrito with fries and a coke." Looking at it once again, he added, "I ... also need a Taco on a Bun, fries, and, uh, a coke."

After Mike gave the man his name, the man nodded and turned to pin up the order for the cook.

"Next."

Karam and Mike returned to the table. Jasmina and Salome were in full dialogue mode but immediately shut down when the men arrived.

Karam asked, "So, what were you ladies chatting about?"

Salome looked at her fiancé and said, "The weather."

Karam looked at Mike and shook his head.

Mike asked, "Does that mean something?"

Karam shrugged and said, "The same thing as talking to my attorney." He saw Mike's frown, "It means mind your own business."

The four of them chatted about work. Karam and Salome's plans for the future. Mike was listening with only one ear. Time was slipping by and he still hadn't figured out how to go about contacting Sarah Bennington, what to say, HOW to say it. His ruminations were interrupted by a shout from the food truck.

"KARAM!"

Karam jumped up, "Here." He walked to the window. Took a few bills from his pocket and then turned to carry his and Salome's meal and drinks back to the table. It was a balancing act but he did it without spilling anything.

After he was seated, Mike said, "Nice job."

"AHMADI!"

Mike got up, "Oh, uh, HERE." He walked to

the window.

The burly man at the window said, "That'll be $23.85."

Mike paused a second then dug his wallet out of his back pocket. *Karam you little …*

After performing his own balancing act returning to the table, he saw Karam's wise-acre grin. Mike shook his head.

He was trying to be miffed at his brother but Karam introducing him to Jasmina was turning into a priceless gift. He was pondering that as he took a bite of his food. His eyes popped open. The food in his mouth muffled the sound somewhat but he managed to say, "This is delicious!"

Karam nodded affirmatively. Both Salome and Jasmina had dug into their food as well. Things went silent for the next five minutes. After disposing of their paper plates and plastic forks, they decided a stroll would be nice to work off some of the dinner. They moved around the seating area by the truck over to a slightly worn path that opened up into a small, presumably community, park. It had a sandy play area on the left hosting a slide, three swings and fake rock sculptures for children to climb. A sprinkling of trees and picnic tables replete with post-mounted barbecues completed the furnishings. The lawn covering the remainder of the park had been freshly mown and the smell of cut grass wafted gently in the air. The sun had set but even with the lamp posts of the park alight, there were a remarkable number of stars visible. It was very unusual, but romantic. Karam and Salome walked in front slowly holding hands. Mike, still wrapped up in his own thoughts, had put his hands in his pockets. His attention, however, was diverted when Jasmina put her arm through his and caressed his bicep with her hand. They looked at each other and smiled.

After completing the route around the park's circumference, the two couples hugged, promised to go on another dinner adventure soon and then bade their goodbyes. Mike and Jasmina watched Karam and Salome take off in Karam's new BMW.

As they got in Mike's car, he said, "I'm thinking of taking wagers on how soon he will have to trade that in for a mini-van." Jasmina giggled. As they started driving, Jasmina noticed that something still seemed to be on Mike's mind.

"Penny for your thoughts?"

Oh, what the hell. What can it hurt to tell her?

Mike explained to her about the trip to the Midwest and his encounter. How it was a request of his dying father to find a certain woman that Mike had never heard of before. All that he had to go on was a tattered photograph. He left out all the gory details of his getting to America and the years it took before finally locating her. He just told her it was many years and he had just about given up when he stumbled across a clue of where to find her. He talked about the near calamity that happened just before he was about to return home.

Jasmina's hand went to her mouth, "Oh! This woman tried to jump in front of a bullet to save you? And on top of that you find out she's your biological mother as well?" She turned and looked straight ahead through the windshield, stunned, her eyes not focused on anything.

"Mike, that is beyond belief."

"Yeah, I know. I feel compelled to contact her, now that the DNA has been confirmed, but don't know what to say or how to word it. Hell, I don't even know what to call her. She's my biological mother. I can't call her Mrs. Bennington or Ms. Bennington, that's too dry and formal. Sarah is too informal … and dry. I don't feel comfortable referring to her as 'mother'. The only mother I've ever known died a year before my father. Both gone just before my twelfth and thirteenth birthdays. At least my mother didn't have to witness all the violence, although the cancer that took her was a poor substitute."

Mike paused and sighed, "Anyway, I need to address Sarah in some manner, but what?" In exasperation he added sarcastically, "Salutations and Felicitations?"

Jasmina paused for a moment and then said, "I'm so sorry to hear about your parents." She paused again to clear her throat, "Well, if it was me, considering the risk Ms. Bennington took, I would feel obligated to say thank you … at the very least."

Mike suddenly tilted his head slightly, "Huh."

"What?"

"You may be onto something."

"Really?"

Mike nodded, "Yes … yes, you've definitely given me an idea." He reached over and took Jasmina's hand in his. "Thank you." He didn't let go the rest of the way home.

Mike walked Jasmina to her front door. They paused while she dug in her purse for her keys. Once she found them, she took them out and said, "Got 'em."

Mike smiled and once again put his arms around her and kissed her deeply, holding her close with his hands now below her waist. Jasmina leaned into him.

When they finally came up for air, Jasmina said, "Thank you for dinner. It was fun … and *very* good."

Mike smiled and replied, "Thank you for … you. I'm already looking forward to the next time I get to see you."

Jasmina's heart skipped a beat, "The only way you won't see me is if you choose not to."

Mike's smile deepened, "Okay, infinity it is."

Jasmina turned, hoping Mike couldn't see the

rush of blood to her face and neck. She fumbled a little getting the key into the lock. After opening the door and stepping inside, she turned and looking out from the half-closed portal, said, "Goodnight, Mike."

"A *very* good night, Jasmina."

Mike turned and walked slowly back to his car. Jasmina shut the door, leaned back against it with her eyes closed and took several deep breaths to get her heart rate under control.

* * *

Both Mike and Jasmina had to work the following morning, and the change in them was noted by their co-workers. When asked what was going on, both of them just smiled and said "Nothing."

Of course, it eventually came out that each had found someone special. Word got around that the confirmed bachelor and confirmed bachelorette had apparently met their match.

CHAPTER THIRTY-SEVEN

Sarah approached the café, parked the car and pondered possible next steps just as she had on the way over to pick up Heather. Her conundrum of how to communicate with her son had not improved since she left the grocery store – still no idea of what to say. She started to get out of the car when she spotted Mark Stoner hurriedly entering the Elkhorn.

I wonder what that's about? I'd better stay put for a few minutes. I'm sure Mark needs to talk with Heather.

* * *

Mark entered the café and looked for Heather. He could see through the passageway to the kitchen that she was hanging up her apron; preparing to leave. He needed to act now. He passed quickly by several tables of smiling customers, giving each a nod on the way. Heather turned to exit the kitchen when she saw Mark only a few feet away and moving quickly toward her.

"Oh, Mark, I … wasn't expecting you." Then with a smile, she added, "But I'm happy to see you."

"Heather, there's something I need to ask you.

It's personal. Can we go into the office for a moment?"

Heather's smile slid down slightly. *Oh dear, what could this be?* An image of the disembodied head of Roger Beaumont floated in her mind. She cleared her throat, "Oh, um, okay, sure."

Mark didn't bother asking his mom or dad. He just took Heather's hand and led her into the office shutting the door behind them. Mabel and Ed looked on. They both expected that soon, items in the office might have to be put back into place. They looked at each other and shrugged.

Mark turned to Heather and said, "Heather, you know how some things need a certain time or a certain place or a certain amount of time or maybe a certain amount of space?"

Heather looked askew at Mark, "No-o-o, what in the world are you talking about?"

Mark felt ridiculous. He cleared *his* throat, "I don't know how things like this are done. I never really thought I would run into anyone as special as you."

Oh my god, is he going to propose?!

"I know … I think … I'm pretty sure where things will end up but maybe now is too soon so maybe it's the right time for an interim step. Do you see what I'm getting at?"

Heather nodded her head once but then shook it twice.

Mark was getting flustered. He decided to just blurt it out, "Heather, I think we should start living together. Will you move in with me … at my place … in my home … with me?"

Heather was shocked, not so much at Mark's question, but that life would have provided such a perfect transition for her moving from a life that was hell to a life with a wonderful man. She stood motionless for several moments.

Mark started to wonder if he had played it wrong. *Maybe she's not ready. I'm a lout, pressuring her like that. What was I think…*

Heather's voice was barely audible, "Yes."

Mark leaned forward, "What was that?"

Her voice got stronger, "Yes, yes, YES!" Heather threw her arms around Mark's neck and kissed him. The momentum nearly sent him backward onto the desk.

"You've made me very happy."

Heather smiled, "Me too."

"Look, I have to go back over to the station and finish up a few things. I'll talk to you in a couple of days about arrangements for you to move in. Okay?"

"Okay," replied Heather, "Love you."

Now it was Mark's turn to smile, "Love you more."

As Mark turned to walk away, he was oblivious of the lipstick on his mouth and totally ignored the giggles of the café customers as he passed by.

Heather smiled and whispered to herself, "Love you most."

Sarah saw Mark Stoner leave the café and get into his cruiser. Since Heather hadn't accompanied him, she made the decision to take up residence at one of the tables near the entrance until the young lady was ready to head home.

After locking the car, Sarah entered the café and found an empty table right by the doorway. She sat down and continued her ruminations on how to go about writing to her son.

It was shortly after Mark left that Heather realized she hadn't clocked out. She turned and walked back to the card rack humming. After stamping her card, she turned around to see Tim Harris. His grin looked like a cat that had caught the proverbial canary.

"Oh, stop that!"

Tim's smile grew larger, "Not on your life, little lady."

Heather shook her head. As she exited the kitchen, she saw Sarah Bennington waiting at a table by the entrance. *Oh, dear. How will I tell Sarah I'm moving out?*

* * *

On the ride back to the farm, Sarah noticed Heather handling the package of bologna. When she relayed the details of her encounter with Melinda and Wayne, Heather started giggling.

"Oh, Sarah, that's priceless."

"Well, I shouldn't have allowed myself to get that upset. It was like I was slandering people."

Heather stopped smiling. Here was a woman that had taken her in and assumed so much responsibility for helping her. Now, she had to tell Sarah she would soon be living by herself on the farm in the very near future. Sarah noticed the change in demeaner.

"Heather? Are you okay?"

"Sarah, I need to tell you something but I worry that it'll upset you."

"Oh, my, dear, please don't fret. You can tell me anything."

They had arrived at the farm's driveway, so Heather paused while Sarah pulled in, came to a stop and turned off the engine.

Heather cleared her throat, "Well, you know from the start that I was working toward being on my own." Sarah nodded. "I've gotten an opportunity … Mark … I have … it's that … " Heather struggled to find words.

"Heather, it's okay, take your time, it's all right."

Heather took a couple of deep breaths, "Mark has asked me to move in with him." The words came out in a rush. A tear started to form in Heather's left eye. She wasn't prepared for the unflinching expression on Sarah's face.

"Well, I know Mark is a good man and he clearly loves you. Is this something you want to do? In your heart? You feel that this is the right thing to do?" Heather nodded.

"Sarah, I know how you must feel about this being … you know … outside of marriage and all."

"Heather, while I understand the church's formal position, I think we all spend too much time telling other people how they should live instead of paying attention to our own lives. Only you truly know if this is the right choice for you. Whatever you choose, you will have my blessing … not that you need it."

"I thought you would be upset … given … you know, that it means you'll be living out here all by yourself."

"Sweetheart, when I first started my journey to return to this farm, I fully expected to be living by myself. It was just a blessing that I met you. Your time here with me has been a gift. Don't you realize that?"

The tears that had started to form were now cascading in free fall down Heather's face, "Oh, Sarah, I love you so much." She hugged Sarah awkwardly in the front seat of the car and Sarah returned the gesture.

"I love you too, dear. I always will. Let's get inside and figure out how to pack you up for your new adventure!"

Heather wiped her cheeks with the heel of her hand, "Okay, that would be great. Mark said it probably won't be for a few days so we have some time. We don't need to rush."

Sarah held up the package of sliced bologna, "Well, maybe that will give us some time to figure out what to do with … this."

CHAPTER THIRTY-EIGHT

The following Friday, Mike invited Jasmina over to his apartment for dinner. He wasn't really a cook but was well-versed in ordering food delivery. The invitation had the added excuse that he wanted Jasmina's help to work on the letter to Sarah Bennington, now that he had mulled over her suggestion. He went through several revisions, but nothing like the tree-killing episode from before. The third revision was read carefully before copying the penciled version in ballpoint pen. Once it was finished, he paused to read the letter aloud. It said,

> Dear Manana,
> If you remember your Pashto, I think you'll understand why I am addressing you in this manner. I hope you are not offended by my not referring to you as

"mother" since the only mother I've ever known, up to now, was during the first twelve years of my life. Even though it's been a long time, I feel I owe her that allegiance as a son.

I have to confess that I was tempted to discard the swabs you sent with me. For that temptation, I can only ask for your forgiveness. I must admit that I was unprepared for the shock upon receiving the DNA test results. I assume your swab tests ended with the same outcome.

Lest I digress further,
I want to let you know
that I intend to stay in
touch. I will come visit
you when it is
convenient for you and
as my time away from
work permits. Please
advise regarding that. I
look forward to your
response.

Very Best Regards,
Michael Ahmadi

After Jasmina arrived, he was anxious to show the letter to her. She put down her purse and pulled out a chair by the dining table and sat down. She frowned with the finger and thumb of her right hand cradling her chin.

"Well, what do you think?"

"Um, it's pretty … terse."

Mike sighed, "It's not like the kind of letter I could write to you, you know, talking about flowers, the sun, the moon. The poetry of your smile."

Jasmina grinned, "Well, I should hope not. She's your mother."

Mike tipped his head slightly to the side, "I know THAT. But that whole…" he started to wave his hands, "… relationship thing is new … and unexpected, at least by me."

Jasmina got up and gave him a hug, "It's a good start. You'll work it out. I believe in you. Maybe you have to proceed in stages."

Mike could feel the tension melt away as he stood wrapped in Jasmina's arms. *How in the world did I get this lucky? Proceed in stages … that's probably not a bad idea.*

* * *

It had only taken a few days for Heather to pull her stuff together but Mark took another week and a half before he deemed his place ready to receive his lady love. Both Sarah and Heather suspected perhaps some house paint might have been involved. But eventually, Heather had moved in with Mark.

Sarah had never seen her happier. Somehow Mark found ways to increase his patrol frequency by the Elkhorn Café which surprised absolutely no one.

Sarah thought that, with Heather no longer at the farm, their encounters would be much less frequent. Things didn't quite turn out that way. Sarah had already had them over for Sunday dinner at least twice. Heather asked Sarah if she could use some of her grandma's recipes. Mark had picked up cooking tips from his parents while attending college, and like the story Heather told her about racing with Mark to replace pillow cases, so it was with meal preparation. The downside of this competition was that they asked Sarah to judge. She asked herself, *I wonder how often parents have to deal with this stuff? The way this is going, my farm will turn into Grand Central Station.* The thought tickled Sarah to no end. Sarah felt she couldn't be happier. She was proven wrong the very next day.

Since the time the lab results had been received, the mail carrier did the routine stop and drive off. And, like the times since, she was again receiving the typical stuff. This day, however, she was sitting in the living room and distinctly heard a double beep. She thought at first that she might have heard someone else's car but a peek out the window caught the mail carrier vehicle driving away. She walked out to the mailbox wondering what could be there. She wasn't expecting anything.

Upon opening the box, she spied one flyer, a gas bill and a business letter sized envelope. The address contained her full name preceded by "Ms." and the street address of the farm. The upper left-hand corner held no name. Just a P.O. Box number and Washington, D.C. completing the return address.

Oh my gosh, it must be from Joseph. Mike, she reminded herself. Sarah tried to remain calm as she once again performed an involuntary speed walk back to the house.

She immediately opened and read the letter, then read it again, and once more. It was both more and less than she had hoped for.

She mumbled to herself, "At least a channel of communication has been opened. Now, my only problem is figuring out how I should respond."

CHAPTER THIRTY-NINE

Mike Ahmadi noticed something unusual upon opening his apartment mailbox. Peeking out was the corner of a fuchsia colored envelope. When pried clear from the other correspondence, it appeared to be the sort that was typical for greeting cards or perhaps some feminine version of stationery. He flipped it over and saw his name and address delicately written by hand. The return address was a Rural Route assigned to Antelope Valley, Oklahoma. It could only have come from one person. At this point, he should not have been nervous, but he was. Mike forced himself to methodically climb the stairs to his apartment and, upon entering, place the mail on the dining room table. He then hung up his jacket and retrieved the letter opener from the entryway table. He sat down and stared a moment at the colorful envelope. After a deep breath and sigh, he opened it and found a sheet of cheap lined paper that had been quarter-folded. He flattened the page on the table and read it.

Dear MJ,

I assume, like me, you were

hesitant to use too formal or too personal a title. It took me a moment of reflection to remember the word manana. I think I understand why you chose it. You are thankful for me (apologies if I'm overstating). Yet, that literal 'Thank You', to an American ear, might be construed as a nickname (of sorts) for mother or possibly even grandmother. Either assumption is fine by me.

I trust you can understand and accept my reference for you. The initials that indicate, by way of your name, two different families and two different cultures, but joined together-in you. I hope this will be acceptable. Time, I guess, will tell.

I am thrilled to hear that you might visit again in the future! That would be more than welcome. I will look forward to seeing you again.

In the meantime, I remain,
your loving,
MANANA

Mike was more than a little surprised by her brief letter. It was almost as short as his, but the surprising part was how familiar the words and expression in the letter felt. *If the situation was reversed, I might well have responded in the same way.* He didn't admit it to himself consciously but the letter was yet another affirmation of their link to each other.

CHAPTER FORTY

The letters continued back and forth between Sarah and Mike Ahmadi. She learned that he had found someone special. Her name was Jasmina. He hoped that, in the not-too-distant future, Sarah would get the opportunity to meet her. Sarah had responded with her happiness that they intended to visit. She shared that the policeman, Mark and his girlfriend Heather had gotten engaged. She also mentioned that she was still tending to her chickens.

After rereading her last letter, it dawned on Sarah that everyone seemed to be moving on to something new; new relationships, new adventures. *Am I going to spend the rest of my life caring for chickens? But, what would I do that would be new, let alone fulfilling, here in Antelope Valley? What would I want to do? What am I QUALIFIED to do?*

Sarah pondered this as she walked to her mailbox to send another letter to MJ and pick up today's mail. After removing the usual flyers and copy of the Antelope Valley Clarion, the local newspaper that somehow had still survived, she placed them under her left arm. She put the letter to her son inside the mailbox and after closing its small door, raised the metal flag on its side upright, alerting the driver that there was something to pick up on the next delivery run.

After getting back to the house and depositing most of the bulk mail in the trash, she made herself a cup of coffee and sat on the living room sofa to peruse the newspaper. When she got to page three, she spotted it. It made her sit upright. *Well, now, if I did THAT wouldn't it be something?* It seemed strange and yet the idea kept bouncing around in her mind. Hmm, maybe *I'll sleep on it tonight and then see in the morning how I feel about pursuing it. The chances of it working out are so slim it probably isn't worth the bother … still.*

* * *

When Sarah woke up, the idea wasn't forgotten. In fact, she realized that it had lodged itself firmly into her brain. It was like an ear worm. If she didn't follow through with finding out about it, it would haunt her forever. She made up her mind. *Nothing ventured, nothing gained.* It was a tired old adage but totally apropos. Now she just needed to find out what the process was to move forward.

* * *

Sarah wondered if her decision was the right one. *Who am I kidding? What makes you think they would want an ex-nun of all things? Well, Sarah, it can't hurt to ask, now can it?* She couldn't decide which introspective-self issued that rhetorical statement, the one dressed in white or the one decked out in red.

She was early for the interview having arrived half an hour early. She was spending most of that time fidgeting and inserting, then removing, the keys to the ignition of her classic car. Jim Johansson over at the Pep Boys had done a fine job getting the car into tip top shape. She had no problems with it since and it was nice to not see the worrisome smoke puff out each time she started it.

She pulled out the ignition key and put the ring of keys into her purse. She took one last look, through the windshield, at Antelope Valley Community Church. She knew that they shared their building with the New Wine Church of Antelope Valley. She had found out that it was a common practice nowadays given the declining numbers and rising costs. She had decided to enroll in a certification program to be an interim pastor. It had taken six months and now that she was certified, she was doubting herself ... again. *Just sitting here is accomplishing nothing. Was that the white angel or the red one? Come on Sarah, get hold of yourself. It's just an interview.*

Exiting the car, she turned to shut the door, having pushed down the lock button before getting out. With a loud sigh, she hooked her purse over her shoulder and began walking to the Administrative Office. After entering the building, she walked a short distance and had to either make a left or right. To the left was the entrance to the Parish Hall, so she knew to turn right. Just before reaching the door with a lighted box above it declaring in red, "EXIT", she noticed the door labeled, "Conference Room". Sarah paused briefly to consider which of the two. She swallowed and chose the latter, knocking lightly.

"Come in," said several voices not entirely in unison.

After opening the door, Sarah took a step

inside and closed the door slowly.

"Hello, my name is Sarah Bennington. I believe I have an interview at this time?"

"Yes, yes," said a rotund gentleman who was at the head of the table, "Please, take a seat."

After Sarah sat down, the man continued, "Let's introduce ourselves." He pointed to the lady sitting at Sarah's immediate left.

"Oh, me first, well, okay. Hello, Sarah, I'm Marcia Cummings, and I'm Secretary of the church board."

Moving one seat further to her left was a somber man, "My name is Phillip Dickenson, and I'm the Treasurer."

The man who started the round robin then spoke, "I'm David Talbot and I'm President of Antelope Valley Community Church." He then turned and looked at the lady to his left. She was very pretty and younger than the others but not by a lot.

"Hello, Sarah, my name is Eunice Dow, and I'm Vice-President of A.V. Community and pleased to meet you."

Sarah smiled and nodded. The man to

Eunice's left was next to speak. Sarah noticed that he sat quite close to Eunice.

"Hi, Sarah, I'm Harold Dow, the lesser half of this partnership." Harold punctuated this with a hitchhiker's thumb aimed at Eunice. Eunice nudged him with her elbow, "Oh, I'm also a member at large on the board."

Sarah couldn't help but grin.

"Sarah," said David Talbot, "we're looking for an interim pastor. Our current pastor is retiring in one month and we are not having any luck with our search", indicating the group at the table, "committee finding a permanent replacement. So, in order to take care of the congregation here and have enough time, God willing, to find a permanent replacement, we've decided on a temporary solution. You do understand that this is not a permanent assignment?"

Sarah nodded, "Yes, yes I do."

"Okay, then, why don't you tell us a little bit about yourself."

"Well, I enrolled seven months ago in a interim pastor certification program and ..."

David interrupted, "Sarah, excuse me, but

we've already reviewed your application and paperwork. What we're interested in is knowing something about you personally."

Sarah squirmed a little then asked, "Oh, uh, so, what do you want to know about … me … personally?"

David could see she was nervous, "Tell you what. How about we use a questionnaire? I found it online and we can go through the questions. If there are any that make you feel uncomfortable, we can either skip them or circle back around later. How's that?"

Sarah decided right then that she liked this David Talbot very much.

"That would be fine, thank you."

Looking at the sheets in front of him, David said, "Okay, then, let's get started."

"What is your favorite part about being a minister and why? Least favorite?"

"I've … I've never been a minister before so I'm not sure how to answer that question."

"Okay, scratch that one." Sarah saw that David meant this literally as he made a small slash mark across the sheet of paper.

"Tell us about your faith journey."

"It's been a very rocky road. Many downs and ups, more the former than the latter."

David was starting to look worried.

"What roles and obligations make up your life? Basically, what we want to know is, how would you balance your personal life with your ministry here?"

"My personal life IS my ministry. It always has been. Ever since I became a novitiate, I've seen no other calling in my life. Except perhaps for this one."

"This isn't on the questionnaire but we do need to ask. Why did you leave the Catholic church?"

"Technically, I didn't leave the church body. I had experienced a traumatic event. I left because I couldn't stay. With the memory of what occurred so present in my mind, I had to get away. I decided to return to the place that had sheltered me in a past tragedy. I abandoned my church. Some would say that I, in effect, excommunicated myself."

Everyone's faces around the table expressed

concern. Sarah wasn't sure whether the concern was for her or against her.

David leaned forward, "Didn't you have a support system? What about your family?"

Sarah decided to just cut to the chase, "My parents were killed in an automobile accident when I was in high school. My grandparents died while I was at GU. I met a man while attending Georgetown whom I loved and thought reciprocated. I got pregnant. He abducted my baby boy and took him to his hometown in Afghanistan. The State Department assured me that I had no chance at recovering him. I was unable to travel there to attempt to retrieve my son. The trauma led to a number of therapy sessions. I decided to join the State Department as the means to an end. While stationed in Pakistan, about twelve years later, I received information that the remaining residents of Mazir-i-Sharif, that was the home town I referenced earlier, had been attacked by Taliban resulting in every man, woman, child and even pets being killed. Believing my son had not survived, I relapsed, left the service and returned to my college town and Georgetown University, the last place I had seen my son alive.

By sheer chance I met a special woman in front of Dahlgren Chapel on the university's campus. She revealed herself to be a nun. Having been raised Catholic, I made the potentially irrational decision to travel with her back to Boston. Shortly afterward I joined her order and took vows. I wanted, I needed, to flee violence. While based in Kansas City, there was an unfortunate incident at the church where I was assigned. A young Hispanic man was holding me at gun point when a detective shot him in the head. I … I left once again because of that."

Harold mumbled, "I'd a thought the shooting at the Elkhorn woulda been the worst." This earned him another elbow from Eunice.

If their chins had been long enough, Sarah would have heard five loud thuds at the end of her remarks. David was at a loss for words. He looked at the sheet in desperation for some way to change the topic.

"Uh, Sarah, um, what do you do for fun?"

After four heads snapped around, their faces stared agape at the President of A.V. Community

Church. David just shrugged and pointed at the questionnaire.

Sarah was the only one with a small smile, "That's a much easier question to answer, my chickens."

"Chickens?!"

Sarah sat up a little straighter and leaned forward, "Yes, the chickens are … residents at the farm I inherited from my grandparents. I give them grain and they give me eggs. Oh, and they're part of my support group as well. I can complain and tell them anything and they'll never squeal on me."

This made everyone chuckle.

David's smile faded as he looked at Sarah, "I'm sorry to ask this but I believe I have to. How can your faith remain strong after the experiences you've had in life? What you just told us would have certainly tested me."

Sarah replied, "Because my son was returned to me. Somehow, a thirteen-year-old boy made his way from Afghanistan down through Iran to the Gulf of Oman, over to the UAE and then to America by way of Germany. And, he did this carrying a college photo of me standing next to his father. I can tell by your faces that you find this incredible. So did he at first. We both submitted DNA tests which confirmed that I am his biological mother."

Once again, it was good that their chins weren't longer.

David gave his head a brief shake and cleared his throat.

"Well, Sarah, how would you envision your role here if you were appointed interim pastor?"

Sarah thought for a second, "To make a difference in people's lives. We need each other in this life. That alone makes all of us invaluable. People need to be reminded sometimes of that fact. They are capable of so much IF they get the proper support, and are willing to support others. Regardless of race, religion, gender or political beliefs, we must not treat each other as enemies, but friends. We must not allow anything to break our bonds of affection toward each other and our faith. We are victorious when we allow ourselves to become the better angels of our nature."

David had two thoughts, *She butchered Lincoln a little bit.* And, *Damn, that was good!*

David turned to the others who had remained silent up to this point, "Any other questions?"

"Yes, I have one," it was spoken by Harold and Phillip simultaneously.

Harold pointed at Phillip and said, "Go ahead. I know what you're going to ask."

"Yes, you do." Turning to Sarah, Phillip asked, "What kind of salary are you looking for?"

Sarah smiled, "Oh, I won't be accepting any salary as interim pastor. I am self-sufficient. I would appreciate coverage of expenses but am guessing that would be minimal."

Phillip frowned, "I don't think that will work. It creates issues. We have to pay your something."

Sarah thought for a second, "All right, you determine what you want the salary to be. Just know that every penny you pay me is going to be donated back to the church."

David couldn't remember the last time that both Harold and Phillip were speechless. He was getting the feeling that they had just uncovered a vein of gold in a dried-up mine.

David said, "Sarah, could you wait outside the

office just for a couple of minutes so we can have a private discussion?"

Sarah nodded, "Certainly. Thank you and it was very nice getting to meet each of you."

After Sarah had closed the door behind her, David looked around the table. He could tell Phillip and Harold had already made up their minds, although he was not so sure of the spiritual nature of their decision.

David looked to his right, "Marcia, what do you think?"

Marcia was staring at the table but then looked up at David's question, "I think it's absolutely amazing that this woman has gone through what she has and still has that kind of positive attitude. And that she feels this is her life's mission. It's incredible."

David turned to his left, "Eunice?"

Eunice looked concerned, "Well, a person goes through that kind of trauma. Who's to say how she'll react if something bad happens around here?"

Marcia snorted, "Eunice, you've got to be kidding me. What could happen around here that this woman hasn't already dealt with in her life? You're the one that's always saying there's no substitute for experience."

David looked at Harold. Harold shook his head, "Nope, not gonna say it. Everybody here is aware of our budget. You all are looking a gift horse in the mouth. I think we have a gem, perhaps in the rough, but a gem nonetheless."

David said, "It's been almost two years to the day that we put out a call." David paused to look around the table, "So, are we in agreement? No need to search for further interviewees?" He looked around the table once again and asked, "All those in favor?"

Eunice spoke up, "Doesn't there have to be a motion?"

Marcia immediately responded, "Oh for pity's sakes. I move we hire Sarah Bennington to be our interim pastor on the spot."

David sighed, "Do we have a second?"

Phillip immediately responded, "Second."

David, "Discussion?"

Marcia, "Call for the motion!"

Phillip, "Second."

David, "We have a call for the motion, all those in favor?"

All said Aye except for Eunice who responded with, "Abstain."

David, "The call for the motion passes. We are now voting on the motion to elect Sarah Bennington as our interim pastor.

"Aye, …Aye, …Aye," David waited a second before adding his own, "Aye … Eunice?"

Eunice's reluctant gesture was followed by a nearly silent, "Aye."

"All right, then, folks. We have an interim pastor and not a moment too soon. Marcia, be sure to document the vote as being unanimous." With that, David got up from the table and proceeded to the door. After exiting the room, he found Sarah down the hallway looking at old pictures of past church functions and membership classes.

He approached her with his hand outstretched. Sarah took it waiting to hear the thank you rejection.

He smiled, "Just wanted to be the first to congratulate you … Pastor Bennington."

Sarah gave a big grin, "Thank you so much. Um, who do I see about next steps."

"Don't worry about anything right now. I'll call you and arrange a time to go over the ins and outs here. We'll have you attend the next board meeting along with the departing pastor. So glad to have you with us."

Sarah smiled and said, "Thank you. I am very much looking forward to being here."

Sarah left and somehow found herself driving home without knowing exactly how she had managed it. She didn't remember anything between leaving the building and finding herself on the road toward home.

How about that. I'm Pastor Bennington now. She wasn't entirely sure how to think about it. It also sank in that now she had to actually perform pastoral duties. Some self-doubt started to creep in but she pushed it away. She was going to celebrate the next phase of her life. *Now, I need to let my son and Heather know about this. I'll bet they'll be as surprised as I am.*

CHAPTER FORTY-ONE

Sarah and Mike Ahmadi had not only gotten accustomed to each other's special names but had also migrated from written letters to weekly phone calls. Each Saturday morning, they would play catch up on what had transpired since the last time that they talked. This Saturday morning ended up being a little different.

"Hello, MJ!"

"Hi, Manana, how are you?"

"I'm fine, thanks. Are you and your friend Jasmina doing okay?"

"We're doing fine. How are your chickens? Has Whitey been behaving?"

"Unfortunately, no. She's pecking at the eggs again. I had to put the wooden ones in the roost. Gosh knows how long I'm going to need to leave them. I think it's definitely going to be longer this time around. Hopefully, she'll get the idea. Only time will tell."

"Until you told me about it, I had no idea that chickens would do that sort of thing."

"Yeah, it happens. So, is work going okay for

you, MJ?"

"Yep, it's good, but busy. They've reduced staff here at the IRS and it's really hindering our ability to maintain oversight and compliance."

"Oh, is your job at risk?"

"Naw, I'm in the policy arm and besides, if something happened, I'd start my own accounting and tax prep business."

Sarah smiled, "Well, you certainly did a fine job with my returns. I've only been getting good news each Spring."

MJ replied, "Oh, speaking of news, I have some but would really like for you to to come to DC in the near future, say, next week or right after that?"

"Oh, MJ, I'm sorry. I have an obligation. In fact, I thought you would have heard about it already. You should have received an invitation in the mail."

"No, I'm sure I haven't received anything like that."

"Well, would it be possible for you to come here at that time?"

"Hm, well, that's kind of cryptic, but … yes, yes, I think I can make that work. Do you want to tell me what this is about?"

"Um, let's have it be a surprise … of sorts. If you haven't gotten the invitation over the next few days, let me know and I'll give you the information over the phone."

Mike Ahmadi laughed, "Okay, a surprise it is. Maybe I'll manage one for you as well."

Sarah smiled, "That would lovely my son. Goodbye, MJ."

"Bye, Manana."

Jasmina walked into Mike's apartment having picked up his mail, "Who was that on the phone?"

"Manana."

"Oh, how is she? Must have been your regular Saturday call." Thumbing through the mail, she added, "Looks like you got a card. Hey, it says it's from Antelope Valley!"

Ahmadi got up and walked over, "Aha! She said I was getting a surprise and mentioned an invitation. This must be it."

He took the card and sat down on a dining room chair. After opening it he said, "Okay, let's see what this is about."

His eyes widened slightly and he went silent for a moment.

Jasmina asked, "What is it? I'm guessing it's the surprise she told you about?"

Mike looked up at Jasmina, "Definitely, and one I would never have guessed in a million years."

He showed her the card.

Antelope Valley Community Church

Proudly announces the installment and inaugural service for our new Interim Pastor – Sarah Bennington

Sunday, July 8th at 9:30 am

217 N. Buchanan
Antelope Valley, OK

Reception to follow service in Fellowship Hall

"Are you going to ask her about this? Seems like a big decision."

"No, but I do need to ask you something."

CHAPTER FORTY-TWO

Now that the surprise had been delivered and Mike realized the nature of the 'obligation' Manana had talked about. He asked Jasmina if they could hold off on the announcement of their engagement until they could surprise his mother in person. Both of them scrambled to arrange vacation time. Mike didn't have much of a lead to arrange airline tickets for the trip to Oklahoma City and summer travel had made locating a rental car in conjunction with the flight a draconian effort.

* * *

Mike and Jasmina ended up getting into Antelope Valley around 9 pm on July 7th. He didn't call feeling it would unnecessarily bother his mother the evening before her big day. He was grateful they had gotten something to eat on the way as it was clear they rolled the streets up early in this town. He was also glad that the promise he made to Sarah, to be on time for her inaugural service, would be met. He wasn't much of a church or mosque attendee but it should be okay. He was familiar enough, thanks to the Syrian Christian family that adopted him and the

Protestant Services he attended. He would get the gist of it. Jasmina was familiar too, although she remained a stalwart agnostic. He sighed, *Tomorrow's going to be a big day for all three of us.*

Before checking into the hotel, Mike warned Jasmina about Donnie and his … mouth. She smiled demurely and nodded.

When they entered with their bags, sure enough, there was Donnie at the desk.

"Can I help you?"

"Yes, reservation under Ahmadi for two. Two nights."

"Okay. Here, please sign in. Do you want to keep charges on the card you phoned in?"

"Yes, please."

"Okay, … here's your key." Donnie took a moment to look at the name again. With a puzzled expression, he asked, "Have you stayed with us here before?"

"Yes, yes, I have."

"Holy Shit, you're Sarah Bennington's son, aren't you ?!"

Mike nodded, but as they started to walk

away, Jasmina added, "You bet your boney ass he is."

Mike tried to stifle his laugh and choked slightly. After getting into their room, he turned to Jasmina, "Jaz, you have *got* to warn me before you do stuff like that. But I have to admit it *was* hilarious. I thought Donnie was going to swallow his tongue!"

She put her arms around Mike's neck, "Sometimes you have to fight fire with fire."

Mike felt his body start to warm, "Or, maybe, heat with heat?"

Using a southern drawl, Jasmina said, "Why, Mistah Ahmadi, what on earth are ya'll suggestin'?"

* * *

The following morning, Mike Ahmadi called Sarah. He hoped he wouldn't be waking her. It was 6 am but it felt like 9. Jet lag hadn't released its grip. True to form, Sarah was already up.

Sarah wondered, *Who could be calling at this hour? MJ's calls on Saturday aren't until 7.*

She answered the phone, "Hello?"

"Manana, it's me."

"Oh, MJ, is everything okay? I was hoping you could be here today."

"It's fine. We're at the hotel giving Donnie elocution lessons." They both chuckled.

"Well, that's a formidable task you've undertaken. Why didn't you come out to the house? We have plenty of room here for the two of you."

"We got in late and I didn't want to disturb you right before your big day."

"Oh, that wasn't necessary. So, what are you up to? Will you get to the service in time?"

"We wouldn't miss it, but there's another reason for my call. Would you be able to meet us for breakfast? I have a surprise for you."

Looking at her watch, she said, "Oh, well, I believe the Elkhorn Café is open right now. I can be there in 30 minutes. Will that work?"

"That would be great but will you have time to prepare before your service?"

"MJ, if nothing else, life has prepared me. If I'm not ready now, it's too late. I'll be fine."

"Okay, then. See you in thirty. Love ya, Bye."

"Love you too, son, bye."

* * *

Mike and Jasmina walked the short distance

from the hotel to the café. They were right on time but could tell that Sarah had already arrived. They spotted her sitting at the second table next to the large front window. The latest tempera art plastered there prevented her eyes from noticing their approach. When they walked in, Sarah smiled and stood to greet them.

"MJ!" Sarah greeted her son and gave him a big hug.

"Manana, this is Jasmina. Jasmina, this is my mother."

Sarah almost stumbled a bit. It was the first time that MJ had referred to her that way. She shook Jasmina's hand and then gave her a gentle hug.

"So pleased to meet you. MJ has talked about you a number of times. You're even more lovely than he described. He told me about the work you do. It sounds fascinating."

"So pleased to meet you too, Ms. Bennington. MJ talks about you often as well. And … about your chickens."

All three briefly chuckled, "Oh, please, Sarah or Manana. Otherwise, I might not know who you're talking to."

Jasmina felt an immediate ease of tension. The lady was so down-to-earth and approachable. Yet, she could tell that Sarah Bennington had waters that ran deep.

As they took their seats, Sarah asked, "So, MJ, what is this surprise you have for me?"

Mike ran through twelve different ways to say it but gave up and simply reached over and took Jasmina's left hand and brought it up to the tabletop. The 3-carat stone shone brilliantly in the sunlight streaming through the window. He then uttered the obvious, "We're engaged. I wanted you to meet your future daughter-in-law."

Sarah stood up and moved over to Jasmina. Leaning down she gave her another hug.

"I am so happy for you both!" She came around Jasmina's chair, leaned down and gave Mike and Jasmina's cheeks a peck. "Congratulations."

Mike cleared his throat, "I didn't want to do this over the phone. I wanted you to meet and hear about the engagement in person. I guess circumstances led to it being on your special day as well. I hope this doesn't interfere with your preparations."

"Nonsense. How could I possibly get more wonderful news on this special day? You have lifted my spirits to new heights. Let's order something to eat and you can tell me all about how you met and what your plans are."

*　*　*

The breakfast lasted an hour but that still left plenty of time before the service. Sarah excused herself in order to prepare for service and deal with any last-minute changes. Mike looked at his watch. They had 90 minutes before the start of the service.

"Guess we can have another cup of tea before heading over to the church."

"Your mother is quite impressive. So approachable but there's much more beneath the surface." After a brief pause Jasmina added, "Do you think she likes me?"

Mike nearly choked on the sip he took, "Are you kidding? She loves you already. Besides, I like you. THAT's what's important."

Jasmina squeezed his hand and smiled, "I like

you a little bit too, mister."

Mike leaned over and gave her a kiss, "Okay, let's go ahead and drive over, maybe take in a little bit of this town on the way."

"Okay, that would be nice."

* * *

Sarah arrived at the church and was shocked that people were already starting to arrive. Pastor Steve Mason was at the sanctuary door already greeting people. He spotted Sarah going in a side door. They looked at each other and Mason gave her a look of bewilderment as if to question why everyone had come so early. Sarah rushed to the pastoral preparation room, donned her vestments and then walked, as quickly as she dared, back around to join the Pastor in greeting congregants.

Mason muttered to Sarah, "Guess your notoriety has gotten around."

Sarah whispered back, "I had no idea." She looked out at the front sidewalk of the church but saw no sign of MJ and Jasmina.

Mason interrupted her thoughts, "You didn't *pay* them to load the pews did you?"

Sarah saw the grin on his face, "No, I didn't even promise them fresh eggs."

Mason chuckled. He had heard about Sarah's chickens. Then he frowned, "You know, when people started arriving, I rushed out here without my notes."

Sarah panicked, "Oh my, so did I!" Just then the organist started playing.

Mason whispered, "We've only got fifteen minutes. Let's go back to my, uh, *your* office and review the order of worship. Make sure you're comfortable with things."

Sarah answered, "That would be great. I left my notes in the prep room. After I gather them, I'll meet you in your office."

"Sounds good, let's go."

They both turned as a space appeared in the line and proceeded down the central aisle. Sarah had her back to the folks in the pews as she and Mason walked quickly to the right and through the doorway to the prep room. Sarah stopped to pick up her notes as Mason went ahead to unlock the office door.

It didn't take too long to review their notes. After the usual announcements and invocation, there would be a hymn. Sally Mayfield was the leader for this particular Sunday and would handle reading the scriptures. Pastor Steve would say a few words and then introduce Sarah as Pastor Bennington who would then deliver the message for the morning. Everything was set.

After locking the office door, Mason and Sarah entered the sanctuary and took their positions at the altar. As Sarah entered, she was unprepared for what was waiting for her.

Seated in the pews were Mother Theresa, the woman she first met at Dahlgren Chapel and who had befriended and supported Sarah for all her years at Saint Ruth's in Kansas City, Mayor Sean Kelly whom she had helped as a young man and who also remained a friend all these years. Next to them was Detective Barry Gentes, the man who saved her from the criminal who threatened her life and by doing so pulled Sarah into the relapse that had sent her back to her home. Next to Barry was his wife, Mackenzie Gentes and, apparently, their baby daughter all dressed up prettily in pink. *How in the world did they hear about this?* Sarah's gaze moved toward the front pews and saw Mark Stoner sitting next to Heather who was smiling and giving her a wink. *That lovely girl somehow managed this!* Sarah smiled back and mouthed a *Thank You.* Sarah then turned her gaze toward the other side and spotted Wayne and Melinda Miller and Ted Torkelson. Melinda gave her a tiny wave.

Two things occurred to Sarah; the pressure was on and she was scrapping her notes. She was going to wing it but she knew what she wanted to say, what she *needed* to say.

She saw MJ and Jasmina walk in just before the doors were closed. *Perhaps they hoped they could slip into the back pews and not be noticed by everyone.* The organist had stopped playing just as they took their seats in the back. The invocation started the service.

* * *

The time for Sarah's portion of the service arrived more quickly than she had anticipated. Pastor Mason had finished thanking the congregation for his years with them, mentioning a few anecdotes that invoked a ripple of laughter. When he turned toward

Sarah, she knew it was time.

"And now our message for today from Pastor Bennington."

* * *

Instead of taking the pulpit, Sarah stood in the middle of the raised platform. Holding her arms out from her sides slightly, Sarah said, "I realize all of us here have something in common. I'm new to this church and we're new to each other. In spite of having a long history with this community, it was long enough in the past that many of you may not know all that much about me. So, I'd like to start by giving you a brief biography."

After about ten minutes, several of the older men in the congregation were starting to experience heavy eyelids, but once Sarah started detailing her experiences in the State Department and then in Pakistan, all eyes were wide open. The story of her trip back home to Antelope Valley provided the segue to the topic she really wanted to speak on.

* * *

"I don't think it's on the church's scriptural calendar for today, but it's very dear and important to me. It's familiar to all of you, I'm sure; The Good Samaritan. I know many of you must be thinking, yes, yes, we've heard it all before. That may be true but what you may have missed, and I certainly missed it the first time I heard the story from Luke, is that it denotes the difference between mercy and compassion."

Sarah took a breath and continued, "Mercy is what we show when someone needs five dollars or when we decide against revenge. A 'quick-fix' so to speak. So, you might say, what does compassion have to do with this? I would ask you to think carefully about what the Samaritan did. Not only did he treat the wounds of the Jewish man, he put him on his pack animal and transported him to a place where he could be taken care of. And, he didn't stop there. He gave the Inn-Keeper money for continued provisions. Even *that* wasn't the final word. He told the Inn-Keeper that he would return with more money if it was needed to care for the man. This is all the more remarkable given that, at that time, the Jewish people and the Samaritans wanted nothing to do with each other.

"Can this 'lesson' apply to us today, in the modern world? As we study the behavior of the Good Samaritan, ask yourself if these qualities are true for you as well. The Samaritan opened his eyes. Three men passed by the critically wounded man. Only the Good Samaritan provided assistance. It illustrates that, before we can help, we must be aware of the need. We need to open our hearts just like the good Samaritan. How differently those three men must have viewed the injured man. That difference was compassion. The Samaritan's heart went out to a helpless, suffering, dying man. It didn't matter that he was a Jew.

"He didn't just feel sorry for this person. Merely treating his wounds and leaving him on the road wouldn't have provided the help the man needed. He didn't leave him alone. He relieved his suffering by pouring oil and wine on his wounds and bandaging them. But if he had merely treated the wounds and left him on the road, it wouldn't have been much help. The good Samaritan was willing to interrupt his travel and offer aid to a needy and helpless man. He put his life on hold for a while in order to do what was more important—show compassion and care to someone in need. What we see here is Christian attitude and action, in a genuine sense.

"I think everyone can agree that now, perhaps more than ever, we don't lack opportunities to be good Samaritans. But we must first see the need, feel compassion, and give of our time and resources.

"Ask yourself these questions. What motivates me to act? What keeps me from helping? At either moment, what is more important than meeting that person's need?

"Lest you think this is solely about money or monetary resources, I want you to know that I personally benefitted from someone granting me a kind word and friendship. Without them taking the time for that simple gesture, I'm sure I would not be here today." Sarah paused to look and smile at Mother Theresa.

"So, how can we use this example? I realize that most if not all of you have helped out your neighbors in time of need. To bring in crops before a storm hits. Provide shelter and safety for loved ones.

But, what are we willing to do for those we … don't like. The others in our community and society that we might not consider friends? Does their ethnicity, nationality, religion or creed disqualify them from our mercy and compassion?"

"You know, at my age, I'm not what some would call 'hip' or 'cool' by the younger generation." This comment brought a few chuckles. Sarah smiled, "And, I would have to agree with them!" Another few mild laughs could be heard.

"I was introduced to an acronym a while back that was new to me. W…W… J …D." A few heads in the congregation nodded. Sarah continued, "What … would … Jesus … do? Maybe that's all we have to remember when we have situations cry out for our help. What would Jesus do? The man who sat down with sinners, tax collectors, and others that their society frowned upon or outright castigated. If he were here instead of me, what would *he* do? What would he have *us* do?"

After a pause, Sarah added, "I want to close with one of my favorite quotes. It's from the writings of Italian author, Luciano De Crescenzo."

"These words will ring ever true for me; **'We are each of us angels with only one wing, and we can only fly by embracing one another.'** Amen."

* * *

Sarah, MJ, Jasmina, Mark Stoner and Heather went to the farm after the service and coffee hour were over. Sarah, MJ and Heather got to chat with each other while Jasmina and Mark flew around the kitchen making brunch. It was a happy, cornerstone day for Sarah's new adventure.

EPILOGUE

"Mommy, when are we going to get there? It's taking so lo-o-ong!" The young girl's head had popped up between the two front seats of the rental car.

"Sarah Jasmina Ahmadi, get back in your seat and put your seatbelt on," her mother said sternly.

"Unnh!" The 11-year-old girl sat back down, re-buckled her seatbelt and stared morosely out her backseat window.

Jasmina turned toward Michael and asked, "Is it much farther?"

Mike Ahmadi glanced at the car's GPS, "When I googled it, it showed that Ranch to Market Rd North 1881 turns into D 1890 just before we make a sharp right-hand turn. After that, it shouldn't be much more."

Jasmina asked, "Where do they come up with these names?"

Mike shrugged, "Beats me."

"I wonder what the 'D' stands for."

Mike half-smiled, "Well, based on the dust

trail we're leaving behind, I'd say 'Dirt' was the likely inspiration." Jasmina smiled.

"Aaaahh!" Sarah Jasmina was swatting at her brother while trying to wipe her left ear. "Joey stuck his wet finger in my ear!"

Jasmina turned in her seat and stared at the 9-year-old with a look that could freeze water, "Joseph Michael Ahmadi, if you don't sit still and leave your sister alone, I'm going to stop this car and deal with you, young man."

Joey stared at the demon who had replaced his mother without blinking. He stayed glued to his seat for the short remainder of the side trip.

As they pulled up to a stop a little way off the road, Sarah Jasmina asked, "Dad, what is this place called again?"

"It's called Baker Lake, sweetie."

"Okay, but why are we here?"

"Let's get out and I'll show you."

The four exited the car. Joey had mostly forgotten his brief brush with death but as a precaution walked by the side of his father and away from his mother and sister.

When they approached the water's edge, Mike turned to his children and said, "Find a flat rock that will fit easily in your hand."

Joey picked up a rock that looked like a pyramid.

Mike smiled, "No, Joey, it needs to be flat on two sides, kind of like a plate, but smaller."

Both Sarah Jasmina and Joey looked around and each quickly found a suitable small stone. When they showed them to their dad, he smiled and nodded. He showed them that he, too, had a flat stone.

"When your grandmother was a little girl, probably a little older than you, Sarah, she would sometimes come by the lake and skip rocks on the water. Like this."

Mike turned and, with a sideways arm throw, sent his stone skittering across the surface. It left behind
eight dissipating rings in the lake.

Joey said, "Wow, good one, Dad."

"You try it, Joey."

Joey's rock managed to make three rings. Disappointment crossed his face as he watched his rings disappear. Just then, Sarah Jasmina threw her rock and managed six rings before her rock finally sank beneath the surface.

By the time the kids grew tired of throwing, Sarah Jasmina had matched her father and Joey had moved up to five. He was getting jealous of his sister but his mother reminded him that as he grew older and stronger, he would probably make more rings than anyone else in the family. That seemed to satisfy him, at least temporarily.

As they walked back to the car, Sarah Jasmina asked, "Dad, do we get to leave now?"

"No, sweetie, we need to stop by the cemetery first."

Joey said, "I don't like that place. It's where you say goodbye."

"Well, Joey," said his mother, "It's also the place that helps you remember. You get to think about the good times you had with that person, the joy they brought to your life. Things like that."

Joey shrugged and nodded.

It was four miles to the cemetery and Mike was anxious to get there. He had found out that his mother's middle name on her headstone had been misspelled.

"I hope they didn't screw up the correction on her gravestone."

Jasmina looked at her husband, "Oh, yes. What was the problem again?"

"They spelled her middle name with a 'Y', can you believe that?"

"We-l-l-l …"

Mike gave a side glance at his wife, "I gave them clear instructions on the phone. They're idiots."

Jasmina decided to wait until they had viewed the gravestone before planning out how she would cool down her husband. Michael Ahmadi could be tolerant of a number of things but incompetence wasn't one of them.

They pulled to a stop between the two gates of the country cemetery yard. Mike and Jasmina had been here several times. First for the funeral and then again, a year later. It had been two years since and through a bunch of screwups, the headstone had finally been placed ten months ago. It was only via web surfing that Michael had come upon the mistake on the gravestone. The name issue had really made him steamed.

The gates were located on the southern half of the cemetery which bracketed a vehicle entrance contiguous with a half-ellipse course to exit. They didn't bother driving in, opting instead to just open the south gate enough to allow passage by foot. When Sarah Jasmina approached the gate, her mother noticed her
feet.

"Sarah Jasmina, you are *not* wearing flip flops in here. Get back to the car and put on your shoes."

"But it's hot and my feet are sweaty."

"Sarah, there are stickers and ant hills in here. You don't want a big ant biting you or stickers in your feet, do you?"

"I'll be careful."

Jasmina paused then said thoughtfully, "Well, let's hope the rattlesnakes are gone this time."

That comment sent Sarah Jasmina jetting back to the car.

She hated snakes and if she had to run, she didn't want to risk tripping in her flip flops.

Joey was inside the gate and shielding his eyes, "Where is it, Dad?"

"It's over in the middle of the northern section but wait for your sister. I want us to go together."

It only took a minute for Sarah Jasmina to put on her socks and shoes and run back to her family. Once they were all inside the cemetery, Mike closed the gate.

"Okay, guys, let's go; it should be over there," he said, pointing north.

When Sarah Jasmina walked ahead of Joey, he noticed she had tucked her pant cuffs inside her socks. He couldn't help but snicker.

Sarah Jasmina sniffed, "Better safe than sorry, moron."

Mike and Jasmina looked at each other and rolled their eyes. The both suspected that in two to three years things were going to get much worse, so they might as well get used to it.

Mike spotted the headstone, "There it is."

They stood as a family and looked over the headstone. Mike was surprised at what a good job the mortuary had done. They filled in and recut the affected portion of the middle name. It was slightly off center, but it helped that the names ran sequentially.

```
RIP

Sarah
Jane
Bennington

An angel with one
wing always willing to
lend so others could fly


b. Nov. 28, 1939
d. August 6, 2016
```

Jasmina hooked her arm through her husband's and gave a gentle squeeze. As she leaned into him, she asked, "Do you think she would have approved of you using gold-leaf in the lettering?"

Mike looked at his wife and grinned, "She would have absolutely hated it." He imitated his mother's voice, "It's much too pretentious!" After a pause he added, "I'm glad the kids got the chance to meet her."

Jasmina nodded, "Yes, it's good for kids to have time with family. I know it meant the world to your mom that we made a point of visiting her."

Mike nodded and then frowned slightly, "I'm not sure Joey will remember much about her. He was only six when she passed."

Jasmina gave her husband's arm another hug, "Well, Sarah Jasmina sure will. That bowl of candy your mother kept on the dining room table will never be forgotten."

That made Mike smile, "Yeah, you're right about that one. I see things in Sarah Jasmina that remind me of my mother."

"Well, then, it's a good thing we named Sarah after her."

After giving his wife a deep kiss, Mike said, "Thank you for that."

Sarah Jasmina made her presence known.

"E-w-w-w! Can we go home now?"

With a melancholy smile, Mike said to his daughter, "Yes, Sarah, we can go home."

Made in the USA
Middletown, DE
26 September 2021